THE
QUONDAM
WIVES

THE
QUONDAM WIVES

A *Novel by* MAIRI
MACINNES

LOUISIANA STATE UNIVERSITY PRESS
Baton Rouge and London

1993

02 01 00 99 98 97 96 95 94 93   5 4 3 2 1

Designer: Glynnis Phoebe
Typeface: Goudy
Typesetter: G & S Typesetters, Inc.
Printer and binder: Thomson-Shore, Inc.

Library of Congress Cataloging-in-Publication Data

McCormick, Mairi.
    The Quondam wives : a novel / by Mairi MacInnes.
      p.   cm.
    ISBN 0–8071–1810–9 (cloth : alk. paper)
    I. Title.
  PS3563.C34458Q6   1993
  813'.54—dc20   92–24432
                                        CIP

Publication of this book has been supported by a grant from the National Endowment for the
Arts in Washington, D. C., a federal agency.

The paper in this book meets the guidelines for permanence and durability of the Committee
on Production Guidelines for Book Longevity of the Council on Library Resources. ∞

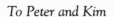

To Peter and Kim

THE
QUONDAM
WIVES

I

It was clearly going to be a bad encounter.

Not only had Alice's hired car lost its aerial to a vandal overnight, but hurtling it through York's medieval streets she brushed a row of parked cars, the hinged mirror on the left side of her car giving a high-five salute to hinged mirrors on their right. The very last car had a rigid mirror and this met Alice's with a clang and shattered. Someone shouted. Alice drove on, her own mirror simply bent back by the impact. She felt gallant and perverse, a Prince Rupert after a cavalry charge that has gone clean through the battlefield and out into the distant countryside. But on the way to Hartland a lorry pursued her so closely that it appeared stuck to her rear window. She bravely slowed down to make the lorry pass her, but it eased even closer, till it fondled the back bumper. As one they neared the Clum turn-off. The lorry driver could not possibly see her signal, so she suddenly accelerated at the last moment and spun off the road into the lane at such speed that her car mounted the bank on the wrong side and only just managed to right itself. The lorry blasted past with a disappointed hiss of brakes.

Falsely relieved, with the lightness of one who has nearly lost everything, she drove into the deep valley where the lovely ruin of Clum Abbey lay and found her old friend Peter Wilson's house looking exactly the same as when it was first built of the abbey stones in 1540 or as she first saw it forty-five years ago.

"Peter, darling!"

"Alice! My dear!"

Each had a good look at wrinkles and sags. They did not have to lie about how much they'd changed. Alice felt relieved to be spared the twenty-minute preliminaries necessary in America before anything taut was said. Nor did she have to say why she was in Yorkshire for an indefinite stay rather than the usual flying visit to her daughters and their families. And yet, schooled in explanation as she'd become, she immediately said that she might stay on and find a cottage and arrange to come for six months of the year, since she was free now. "I'm that age," she told Peter Wilson.

He looked perplexed. It was exactly then that the encounter went bad.

"Free? You're free? Surely it's not your age, Alice, that lets you be free. That suggests you're beyond it. You're not, are you? You don't look it. You're absolutely glowing, Alice. And you haven't exactly lost your figure, have you? If I may say so to an old friend, it's your taste in men that's let you down." He meant it lightly. He smiled at her winningly.

But Alice was outraged. "*What* taste? You sound as if I were Catherine the Great."

"That fellow in New York . . ."

"Bob?"

"That fellow Bob . . ."

"Robert Winship is his proper name. Call him Robert Winship."

"You thought that Robert Winship might turn out well if you worked on him? He was in love with you, so that gave you enough power, you thought, to tidy him up? The way you worked on Anthony?"

"Total crap. And how dare you."

"Surely I can be personal with you, Alice, after all these years!"

"Absolutely not. I was simply explaining the minimum. It occurred to me that as a matter of courtesy I should let you know why I was not in my usual breakneck hurry to go back to New York. My God." Alice stood up and gathered her gloves and her bag. She had been there half an hour.

"Alice? I don't think you've explained a thing. And, Alice, you're very bossy, you know that. Alice Bossy Boots. Oh, come on, Alice. You were always one for running people."

She sat down, but kept her bag and her gloves on her lap. "I thought I owed you an explanation, that's all. I had no idea we'd be having this sort of conversation, or I wouldn't have come." She softened, as always after a display of tartness. Life was more complicated than tartness recognised. "And yet, do you know, I dreaded that it might happen. Something's going wrong between you and me this very minute. What is it, I wonder? Something to do with Jess's death."

"Well, of course, Alice."

"Oh dear, I am so very sorry, Peter, it must be ghastly. I can feel her here now." They both sat back and for a silent minute dropped tears for his wife, who had died of a heart attack a year ago. To be kind, Alice asked meekly if Peter really meant it about her bossing her lovers into neatness. But before he could answer, tears again rose to her eyes and she despaired and looked out of the window. "What a marvellous view that is over your fields up to Copper Nab. I'd forgotten."

"Well." He was awkward, widower-like. He offered her another sherry and stood in front of her, wistful. "You'll stay to lunch, won't you? They leave it in the kitchen for me."

"They?"

"They." He looked belligerent.

She did not want to think of having lunch with him. "The women of our generation were brought up to please, weren't they—I wanted to please simply because that was the way I was brought up. English hypocrisy—*Thank you so much. How kind. What lovely flowers. What a delicious meal. How nice you look. So sweet of you:* when what you mean is, go and be happy, damn your eyes, but bloody well leave me alone. Why don't we face up to things?"

After a shocked pause, Peter said, "Jess faced up to things. She looked life in the face. Then she looked death in the face."

"She was a brave woman, was Jess. I always thought so."

"Had to be brave, married to me, you mean? Well, there's always reason to be low, isn't there, but Jess got *very* low. Finally she had to look for help. She was in therapy when she died. With Gwen as a matter of fact."

Alice was amazed. "Gwen hasn't said anything to me."

"She wouldn't, would she?"

"I suppose not."

"Jess enjoyed her therapy."

"I wonder why she got low. Though it's common nowadays."

"As opposed to the Middle Ages, say? At the time of the Black Death? I suppose you notice how many people are low if you believe that we're supposed to be happy."

"Well, aren't we?"

"No, of course not."

"Do you think we create the taste by which we are appreciated?" Alice asked, still humble.

"So it's our choice, you mean?"

"Of course."

"Jess cried a lot in her therapy."

"I thought you said she enjoyed it?"

"You can enjoy crying, surely."

"I suppose so, given a certain amount of bottling up beforehand. Poor Jess."

After that, there was no alternative; she had to stay to lunch.

The farmhouse had once been the manor and still kept a room with a hearth big enough to house a family and its servants on cold winter nights. It now accommodated an Aga, bright red, and a black Victorian cast-iron range. Before it they sat in warmth, and Peter lifted the covers on a half-carved ham, a sliced tongue, a game pie, and some cheeses on a board, all set out ready on a clean linen cloth. They started with a soup made of green vegetables. Gretchen had made it—Gretchen, his son Calvert's wife. They lived in another part of the house, and had done so since Jess died. Calvert ran the farm now, with Peter as his helper.

"You can't tell me it works," Alice said.

"Yes, it works quite well."

"Sharing the house, sharing the farm?"

"Yes."

"Gretchen doesn't mind having you here?"

"No, why should she?"

"I minded Lady Stella being there when I married Anthony. She was there over thirty years after the death of the father, as you know. She wasn't going to slip down the road and live somewhere else. Anyway, of course the house was vast. There was plenty of room. I thought it was her fault, though, that our marriage started off on the wrong foot. I was totally wrong. It was the hall's fault, not Lady Stella's."

"Well, they can't blame me," Peter Wilson said. "I do as Gretchen tells me, I go to bed early, I eat what is put in front of me, I live in my own rooms . . ."

"How boring of you."

"Yes."

"Where are they now—Calvert and Gretchen?"

"I've no idea."

"So it can work?"

"Oh yes."

"I fought that place," said Alice, "and it won. I'd no idea till I got there what I had taken on. I'd married Anthony so blithely. Everyone was delighted, a splendid match my mother said, so much better than that other creep—that married creep—I'd been seeing. What a good-looking man Anthony was, a gentlemanly man, a man of breeding, a man of background, oh bugger it all. Couldn't go wrong. 'So what if he's county,' my father said, 'you can cope with that, they're dodoes and they know it, those people, the county families. The point is,' he said, 'you'll have the *freedom* to do as you want.'"

Alice screamed softly. "No one had the common decency to say that I was really marrying a huge broken-down mansion with no central heating, barely adequate plumbing, defective lighting, and leaks in the roof. No one said, 'Girl, you've thrown away your youth on stone and slate.' All they said was, 'Anthony adores that house of his, doesn't he?' 'Of course,' I said, 'he has such marvellous taste.' And, poor booby that I was, I really looked forward to getting the place in some order. 'It's been allowed to run down,' I said to all the kind friends and neighbours. And *they* said—and I'm sure you were among them—'Yes, love, Lady Stella has let it go, and so did Anthony's grandfather, it got away from them,' and they bit their lips, these friends did, and looked strange. Because, you see, they hadn't the guts to tell me that it required an injection of several million pounds and an army of workmen to be rehabilitated, let alone brought up to date, and Anthony and his mother simply didn't have that sort of money. It wasn't for years and years that I realised that my bucketsful of tears and screams of rage were due to frustration over the hall. Do you know

5

what I'm saying? In that bloody house nothing *worked*. And no one told me that I had no right to expect anything to work. Not Lady Stella, poor old fruit, not Anthony, of course, and not even you, Peter dear. Ah me." Tears once more streamed down Alice's face.

A pause. Peter fidgeted. How to stop the awkwardness? He asked kindly, "Who was the married creep?"

"That is not the point. Very well, these days he's quite a well-known old fart on the box."

"You'll be calling me an old fart next."

"I might well." Alice sighed. "How beautiful it is in this part of the world. Why don't I come and live here in a house that works. Would I go mad?" She made the question an insult.

Wounded, Peter said, "Speaking as an old fart, I can only say that I love it," and to his relief Alice smiled warmly at him.

"I was obsessed with order," she explained, as if he'd asked about it. "I had to put everything in order—fight the inertia of the past and put life in it. Children, you know: poor Gwen and Reggie. And of course, those sons I never had. Bloody place, it won. You know that, don't you? Quondam Hall won. I wish I'd known what I was getting into when I took Anthony on. He wasn't the sort of man I'd planned on marrying. I wanted to do something worthwhile with my life. God, how boring for you to have to listen to this. But it's true—Anthony was an aberration. Why did I marry an aberration? I've often wondered. Do we choose our partners, or are we just careless? Do we repeat the pattern of our parents, or try to correct it, or what? I mean, Robert Winship is not like Anthony, so you need not go on about my wanting to do something or other with great powerful men. They're quite different kinds of men. Anyway—I've always been orderly; my parents brought me up like that. Untidiness was the mark of a second-rate mind. Cool quiet authority was what I went for: formulas for tackling large difficult situations, together with wit and readiness for chaos. That propensity of mine, it attracted the oddest men. I didn't care so long as they were really intelligent and witty.

"So I was seeing Charlie Pogmore—yes, the man on the box, the celebrity. You know him, yes, you know the man, you don't care for what you know, you are right, he's a toad. But wonderfully intelligent, Peter, and witty, and very funny. Not like Anthony. I've always found

6

intelligence to be sexy, the sexiest attribute of all. Intelligent of him to like me, for example. He wanted to get into Parliament when I knew him. I was madly in love with him. He must have known. He was married, so I didn't say anything, but he knew. He had a wonderful gaunt face. He was as thin as a rail. Not the toad features of today. Well: I was seeing them both. Anthony asked me out to dinner. I put on my little black dress and he took me to Prunier's or the Cafe Royal or some nice little place he'd heard about—always somewhere very nice, with atmosphere and excellent food. I liked Anthony a great deal. A charming man, a powerful figure, a man of authority. I looked up to him. Not the undercutting sly funny toad that Pogmore was in his youth. At the time Anthony reminded me of a very good suit that you never look forward to wearing. Meanwhile I canvassed Bexleyheath with Charlie the would-be M.P. One day we were in a railway carriage together going down there. On a Saturday I think it was. I was a student at the LSE then and wasn't free in the week. It was midmorning and the train was empty and we had the compartment to ourselves, sitting opposite each other, and Charlie began to question me about my view of the Labour Party, would I really put my life on the line for them. So, 'Yes,' I said indignantly, 'of course, that's what I'm here for' (a lie). And he said quite suddenly that of course it wasn't his business. He may have been checking me out for suitability as a politician's mate. Anyway, to my shame and horror he burst into tears and asked me to marry him the moment he was free."

"Good God."

"Of course, I said, of course, I can't wait. He then left his seat opposite me and crossed over and sat down beside me. I expected to hug and kiss. I loved the man." Alice began to laugh. "You will never believe this. All he did was to hoot and chortle and gather his legs under him on the seat and snuggle up to me like a puppy dog. I felt a perfect fool. When we arrived at Bexleyheath, there was his agent on the platform with a bunch of leaflets. Charlie was ecstatic. His eyes shone. I felt ecstatic too, but under the ecstasy I was ashamed of him. What a cardigan, what a piece of badly knitted home produce! Yes, we became lovers. I couldn't believe I'd seen the real Charlie in that train. But I had. I went on being ashamed of him all the time, even at our best moments. He was an embarrassingly bad lover, too. That was the worst. So eventually Anthony asked me out to dinner again—he knew nothing of Charlie, mind you—and we went to a nice little place in Soho and he proposed to me, and I sat in my little black dress and said yes."

Peter Wilson considered this ancient tale. His face had gone red with jealousy. Alice saw and didn't care. He got up and smiled and started making coffee.

After a couple of minutes' silence, Alice felt it behoved her to find common ground. "You know what passion is, Peter."

"We all know about passion."

"I always thought—Esmé." Esmé was Anthony Quondam's second wife, whom he had married at the age of fifty-four, when she was a young girl.

"Yes! You saw that? I hoped it wouldn't show. Long ago, of course. I don't understand it now. She reminds me of a Pekingese."

"Why not a Pekingese? I had Charlie. So you felt mad about Esmé. Well. I think that's admirable. So instead of Charlie I married a pile of stones."

"Come, Alice, how you exaggerate!"

"That's what Anthony used to say."

Peter pondered the story as a friend will, not so much for itself as for the light it throws on the speaker. Her rows with Anthony Quondam were famous.

"How does Esmé cope?" asked Alice. "He doesn't bully her, does he? I never see her, you know. I hear about her from the girls, but I haven't seen her for years."

"You get on, don't you?"

"I suppose we get on."

"She wants to see you."

"What on earth for?"

"Really, Alice."

"It is not natural for the two wives of one man to get on well together. Unless they're Muslims," she added scrupulously. She frowned. "Even then there must be a certain amount of jealousy. Or a completely different attitude from ours. I dare say that if the two wives both adore the ground their man walks on, they get along nicely. Though there again . . ."

"Oh Alice, do stop!" Alice stopped. Peter went on: "Esmé wants Anthony to turn the estate and the hall over to the girls. Now, at this very moment. She's been on at him to do so for years. Has Gwen told you? Or Reggie? Come to think of it, they may not know. This month Anthony turns eighty, and it seems quite reasonable to choose this moment to retire to Akeld, out of the picture, and let the girls take over. Esmé wants your Gwen and Reggie and her Delia to split the hall between them and live there together. Well, Delia's living there already, as you know. She uses the old barn as a studio. Anthony has rigged it out for her. Has Gwennie told you? Delia came back from university with some idea that she had to paint, as an antidote to the rationality of the university. She's been lucky, won some sort of prize run by a London gallery for young people. They like having her at home. A good thing to use some of the space intelligently, Esmé says. In fact it gave her the notion that your daughters and their families could use the rest of the space more profitably than Anthony and herself. Anyway, Esmé wants you on her side, to help persuade Anthony that a transfer of the hall and estate will benefit everybody."

"Poor Anthony! Why should he leave his beloved hall just for the sake of Esmé? He loves that house."

"I thought you hated it."

"For myself. It ruined my life."

"Then you must feel for Esmé. Surely you see how much more comfortable she and Anthony will be at Akeld. Esmé's going to put in central heating, which will suit his arthritis, and she plans to have the main bedroom on the ground floor."

"What on earth will he do there?"

"He's going to write that famous local history of his."

"That's all very well, but Quondam Hall is his home, his family's lived there for hundreds of years. It's not just a flat or a cottage or a house that catches your fancy and you get a mortgage for it and move in and fill it with your gear. It's a beautiful old hall that's been loved and lived in and died in and treasured, that gives shelter and authority and responsibility to its master and mistress and a roof to their children and dependents, summer and winter, summer and winter, for year after year after year. You don't just throw it away because your bones ache a bit and it gives your wife chilblains. Its foundations are

9

his foundations, its paths and gardens are the stuff of his childhood, its walls are his limits. The hall is himself, his whole self. I've no time for the landed gentry, God knows," Alice continued with a glare. "They're not worthy of their possessions, ninety-nine times out of a hundred. But houses—or ideal houses—are important. Anthony can arrange to give the girls the hall now and to live in a corner of it for the remainder of his lifetime. It's not entailed, I know for a fact. He can do with it as he pleases. There's no need for him to move out."

"A bit of the hypocrite, aren't you, Alice?"

"No I'm not. I'm thinking about Anthony. I got out so Anthony could go on being Anthony. I don't want the man I left to change into a merely rational human being."

"Anthony has more humanity than any man I know."

"But is he rational?"

"He's more than rational, dear thing."

"Susceptible, you mean, don't you?"

"Honestly, Alice!" Though he laughed, Peter had to refrain from agreeing with her. She was far too bumptious already. He decided to speak of practical matters, thinking that Alice the businesswoman would respond. "Then there's the money side of it. Esmé says that Gwen and Reggie can afford to pay into the hall what they now spend on two separate households. She says she doesn't know how she and Anthony can afford to live there any longer. The estate barely turns a profit these days. It's soaked up her money, she says, just as it soaked up Lady Stella's. The hall has depended on dowries far too long."

"Possibly. But Gwen and Reggie don't have the mental equipment demanded by the hall. Even though they spent their childhood there. They were away in their adolescence, when they became aware. They don't know the hall, and the hall doesn't know them. Delia's different. She's lived there all her life."

"You have a rare old theory about that hall of yours."

"One learns about the importance of theory in America. Everything has its theory there. Theories are a lot of fun."

"So it's no use asking you to back Esmé?"

"What good will I do? Besides, I have hardly seen Anthony and Esmé since I put them up in New York ten or twelve years ago. As you know. And what a farce that was. Anthony behaved appallingly to everyone, just because the customs men had been rude to him at JFK. Customs people are rude to everybody, it's a rule of life. Winship left town till I sent Anthony to Florida, which of course he adored."

"There was some talk of his retiring there."

"Has everyone gone mad?"

Peter Wilson's farmhouse backed on to the only street of Clum. The village lay on a ridge overlooking Swathbeck Vale on one side and on the other a narrow valley with steep wooded sides and a floor of fields. A brotherhood of streams ran through the valley. Here to one side lay the ruined abbey that had brought the village into being. Peter Wilson's house was only slightly bigger and more prosperous than the other houses. It was built of the same stone, and had the same greenish Westmorland slate roof that a generous Quondam landlord had put on all dozen houses there two centuries ago. The Wilsons, father and son, kept a thousand sheep on the moors and in local fields, a flock of poultry in the yard, and a patch of vegetables and cutting flowers nearby. Peter in his sixties was a broad, big-handed man with a reddened face and white thinning hair. Alice, leaving, backing her car carefully between stone walls with their crust of bushes, thought that there couldn't be a gentler light than that which flooded the sombre wooded sides of the valley. Standing in it, waving, Peter looked somehow younger and saintlier than she knew him to be. And Alice reckoned that she herself must look tawdrier, after her sojourn in wicked New York.

She blew a kiss, changed gear, and slipped down to the abbey ruins for another look. Once upon a time, William the Conqueror had laid waste this countryside in the famous harrying of the north. Not a village or town remained standing between York and Durham. Crops were burnt and livestock killed. People died of starvation, their mouths full of grass. After fifty years of wilderness, monks in white habits walked in, sent by St. Bernard from Burgundy to live in the simplest and hardest conditions. A long time had passed, but something absolutely exhausted still seemed to pin the place down. A simple place. An old place, now green and wooded and visited by people in gaudy leisure clothes and huge white running shoes. Clum had once been Anthony's, and it would be still if it hadn't been for Alice. God forgive me, Alice said to herself as she looked about her. Now it was Peter's; it stayed the same. If it were still Anthony's, he might well put a supermarket next to the abbey, given his present unpredictable desire for change.

And then she thought of Delia, Esmé's child by Anthony. What was Delia like? How interesting to have a child who wanted to be a painter. Alice's daughters had no talent of that kind whatsoever. Oh, Reggie once fancied herself on the piano, but stoutly as Alice applauded her performances at school concerts and sought out the best teachers for her, her musical ability died of its owner's neglect.

And what did Delia look like? As a child she was skinny. Alice's daughters were not at all good-looking. They were nice women, but not good-looking. Alice knew she herself was good-looking. Anthony was good-looking. What had happened to poor Gwen and Reggie for them to be so plain? It is my fault, Alice thought: it is the divorce, it is the misery that children suffer through divorce. "She's very lovely, you know," Gwen had said of Delia, her half sister, eighteen years her junior. Alice took this as a species of generosity.

"I could easily live here," Alice said aloud, driving to Hartland from Clum. She thought she might look incognito at Quondam Hall and imagine living there again. Reality would make it impossible. Impossibly bad taste, with Anthony and Esmé alive and nearby. And who would want to live in that frightful house again, after all she'd gone through. But just supposing Gwen and Reggie took up the idea of residence there, and supposing they got grants and whatnot to do it up and open it to the public, might not Alice take tea there, take a look at what was going on, man the gift shop, dig in the kitchen garden, do the accounts? Hush, she told herself. Such thoughts were dreadful. She would merely drive to Hartland on this occasion and take a look at Quondam Hall. But she repeated to herself that she could easily live here. She looked back on the valley and its ruin. Then the lane crossed ploughed fields where rooks and sea gulls were feeding. The hedges were still red with haws. Clouds proceeded eastwards, the special English clouds that you never saw in New York.

Hartland was a big village with a full range of shops, such as an ironmonger's, a chemist's, a bakery, two butcher's, a grocer's, a video shop, a stationer's, an antique shop, a bookshop, and a shop for country wear, as well as (ominously) three gift shops. There were also three pubs and two cafes. All these lay on three sides of the square where the market was held every Wednesday. Quondam Hall occupied the north side, separated from the square by a stream that ambled through the village from one end to the other, and by the road leading to the moors and the cities beyond. The great stone house lay behind a high stone wall pierced in two places for simple gates to a forecourt. Vehicles nowadays came to a side entrance, but it was possible to walk in from the pavement past the loops of a cast-iron chain strung between cast-iron posts, all painted glossy black, to the front entrance, a simple dignified arrangement with a pair of stone steps up to meet a pair of columns on either side, with ionic capitals supporting a handsome pediment. The door itself was painted midnight black, with a small brass knob. On either side stretched three bays with tall windows in walls of creamy local stone crumbling on the lower reaches. Inside, Alice knew, were all the huge freezing stately rooms that the exterior implied, the endless dark and dirty passages, the rotting silk curtains and falling plaster and worn carpets that devotees of such houses have come to expect. She had no doubt that the house had deteriorated further since her day. She recalled its impact in the days when Anthony's mother was still alive, the impression of its proportion and scale.

In her twelve years of marriage to Anthony, Alice had come to know everyone in Hartland very well indeed. After the divorce she hadn't made herself known there for ten years. The girls paid frequent visits, of course, but she'd dropped them off in the square and vanished without greetings, not pausing even to shop, rushing back to her house in York. When Gwen and Reggie married and she moved to London, she returned to visit them and her friends almost as if she were disgraced. She still felt some regard for Esmé and the proprieties, but who would recognise her now? She parked her car in the square and was swept with a wave of freedom. Should she send a postcard to Bob in Maine, where he'd gone hunting? Should she apologise for her unkind remarks and the exasperation with him that had eaten away at their contentment with each other? Should she beg him to resume their life together? No, that was the wrong expression. She might say that she was lonely and contrite and that she missed him terribly. Then she decided that she would send a card to her business partner, Roz Blair, instead. But she went into the post-office more out of bravado than a wish for postcards of Hartland's market cross and over-restored church. The man in charge gave her a bright blue-eyed appraisal like a bank manager's, and a crisp "Good afternoon" in a manner very different from that of the deferential, slow-witted portentous Ron Harrison, who'd been postmaster in her day. She chatted to him a few minutes, bought some stamps and postcards, and was leaving, amused and satisfied, when heels came cracking along the pavement towards her and a woman cried, "Eh, Alice, is that you?"

At first Alice couldn't recognise the big, rough red face, the dark eyes, the heavy black brows and shock of dark hair, the dark down on the upper lip and cheeks. "It's Sally," the woman reproached her. "Sally Ayton."

Alice had inherited responsibility for the local cell of the Women's Institute from her mother-in-law when she moved into the hall, and that was where she first met Sally Ayton. Old Lady Stella had run the local women like a regimental sergeant-major. If a woman failed to show up for a meeting, Lady Stella was round at her house the next day inquiring if there was illness in the family. Alice was nonmilitant. Good housewifery was a virtue in others, nothing to practise herself. She went so far as to be friendly, helpful, and sympathetic to the members of the W.I. Esmé, she heard, actually refused to have anything to do with such a comic institution. The days of patronage and milady were past. Every woman for herself, said Esmé in her delicate, slightly fey Scottish precision. If the women of Hartland wanted a W.I., let them run it themselves. So the W.I. died in Hartland. A pity, people said. The old solidarity among all kinds and conditions of women vanished. Then there was talk of the younger women having jobs, and cars to get to the jobs, and of wider interests, and of labour-saving devices taking the place of the old skills, and of greater companionship with men. Mrs. Ayton was the wife of a leading farmer. "Alice, it is you, isn't it? I'd know you anywhere. You haven't changed really. A bit o' white in your hair, that's all. Eh we've missed you!" She threw her arms round Alice and hugged her to her soft bosom.

Alice had smiled, had been about to speak, but the embrace startled her.

"You know, I was thinking about you," Sally Ayton went on, unperturbed by her speechlessness. "I was thinking we'd see you, now Anthony's giving up the hall to the girls. 'Perhaps she'll come and live there,' I said, 'now Anthony's leaving, and Esmé. We could do with Alice,' I said. 'We know where we are with her.'"

"That would be quite impossible, Sally. I shall never, never come back, it would be quite wrong in every sense, you know that. And anyway, none of this has been decided."

"Of course it's decided. Esmé told me herself."

"The girls haven't been told yet."

"Get away with you!" Mrs. Ayton's life was all of a piece, and Alice's reappearance was nothing out of the way, and the imminent occupation of the hall by the daughters who had left long ago was merely the bonanza of living long enough to see it happen. "Of course, Anthony's old, and I can see he wants to retire like other men, but he shouldn't leave the hall now, Alice! I suppose I shouldn't say it, and I'll be glad to see the girls back at the hall with their families, but for Anthony I've never heard of anything so daft in all my life."

So Sally's talk of Alice's return had been just flattery! Nothing compared with the threat that Anthony himself might go. But both events were highly imaginary for Sally Ayton. Alice had been a perfectly happy revenant a few minutes ago. Now she was presented with the need to make a solid and practical judgment, at which she promptly failed: "I think you are right about Anthony, but I don't think I can do much about it." What a very English and inadequately human answer!

Sally Ayton stepped back as if reproved. "Well, you're looking very bonny, and I wish you were still here and we wouldn't have any of this silly business. I've never felt right with Esmé. I don't know where I am with her. We all feel we're being swept aside. We have no say."

"Sally . . ."

"You think I'm going over the top? But your daughters are going to share it, aren't they, with Delia? They'll listen to you."

"It's not my business, Sally. Put it out of your mind, Sally. I have a business in New York, and a life of my own there."

"A nice man, Alice? As for the other, it's like I say, Esmé's sweet. Anthony spoils her and she's never content. But is she any use to him, Alice?"

Alice made an enormous effort. "You don't mean in bed?"

"Ooh, we've missed you, Alice! What a thing to say! But you are right, he's an old man, she's still young."

"I don't know what his needs are. What do you call 'need,' these days?"

Anthony used to tell her that his character was at odds with his heritage. Did the conflict make him more, or less, human? He was thwarted, yes. He was privileged, yes. Perhaps his humanity, so much praised by Peter Wilson, came directly from the clash?

Alice had never been given to self-doubt. As she drove on to York and her daughter Gwen's house, she uncharacteristically wondered whether there was a proper way to behave in these extraordinary circumstances. When she arrived in Hartland to start her new life after her wedding in Norfolk and her honeymoon in Rome, she looked forward to it as she looked forward to starting a novel by Trollope. She'd always admired how finely people in her new position behaved in his pages. They considered, made up their minds, and stuck to their decisions no matter how inconvenient; or else, having considered and reached no conclusion, went away in order not to embarrass their friends. Alice was sure that given Anthony, Quondam Hall, and Hartland, her behaviour would be equally delicate and good and brave. Instead of being crass or stupid or muddled, she'd have time and space to be admirable.

Unfortunately, she recognised very little of Trollope's world in the Yorkshire of the fifties. The gentleness survived, but it was minor and weakly. The war had seen to that. On the other hand, the war had confirmed Anthony's enjoyment of power and popularity. Alice watched him from the sidelines with despicable resentment. Then one day, when they'd been married about a dozen years and not happily, Anthony had come to her and offered to reform. "Look," he said, "I swear I'll be faithful to you and I'll give up betting, and let us have more children. I think you should have a son." He kissed her gently and then more ardently and at last with passion. And Alice, instead of yielding and laughing, thought only how full of himself he was, and she kicked and struggled and shouted that if he'd wanted a bloody son, he should have been nicer to her all along, it was too late now. So Anthony went off to the York races and lost £30,000. It was a famous spectacle and left most people speechless. Thirty thousand was a lot of money in those days, and he couldn't raise it from the bank. So he sold the Clum estate to Peter Wilson for that amount and paid the bookies. You might say it happened because Alice didn't know how to behave.

Though there was more to it than that. Not only did Alice resent his power, she also came to think that Trollopian manners, what was left of them, were downright inappropriate. Lady Stella said, "You must treat everyone in the village in the same way. No favourites. Be friendly and kind to all. That's how we do things here." Under such a system, there could be no finely considered behaviour, only a bland sweetness. When Alice came back during visits from America in the early seventies, she saw that a great levelling had taken place and a consequent release of social energy, and she was relieved. That era passed as well. By now, Trollope's world was bones in the desert: who was to pick them up and identify them? Not Gwen and Reggie. Delia, then? Anthony himself? She had married a vigorous, well-educated man of the world who had been an outstanding soldier and who became a remarkable backbencher. He was a man who got things done, a man who solved people's problems and had his say in the national forum. Was he now, in his old age, to become just another loony with a notebook, fitting past lives into a vicar's local history? Such crap, Alice said to herself, that's not for Anthony.

2

Alice and Anthony's elder daughter Gwen counselled for a living. People came to see her who were suffering traumas of bereavement, marital infidelity, divorce, bankruptcy, alienation, miscarriage of justice, and so on, and she listened to them carefully and asked questions till their situations became clearer to them. Often that was enough to restore them. If it wasn't, she made a few sensible small suggestions on how they might modify their behaviour, or other people's, to the end that life might become more comfortable. "Are you comfortable with that idea?" she would ask; often they agreed, surprised to find that comfort could be reached through living with an idea. Her great strength lay in the little she said, rather than the originality of her advice. "Have you tried not answering him?" she asked the wife of a man who provoked shouting matches that ended in blows. "Have you tried saying, 'I feel like a walk. Would you like to come? We could talk things out as we go.' He is unlikely to shout at you in the street and knock you down." Often the patient was so amazed at the dullness of what she proposed that he would feel reassured. He could have thought of that for himself. People with more difficult and intractable pains she referred to doctors, lawyers, the police, explaining to the patients that they had to choose how they were to be made whole. Because she made no bones about the little she was capable of, and respected those who came to her, she helped many people who were in despair.

She lived with her husband Billy Bowers and their son and daughter in a tall Victorian terrace house of dark brick on the west side of York, just outside the walls of the medieval town. Her consulting room was on the ground floor. The upper floors belonged to the family. Billy Bowers ran a furniture workshop in the basement, where he and a workman restored antique furniture bought at auction in market towns in the dales. These, together with new pieces improvised out of old ones, he sold in an expensive shop in Harrogate at high prices.

The division of the house in its present fashion seemed cleverer a dozen years ago, when the Bowers family first moved there, than it did now. It seemed utopian then just to have space and order for parents and children. Now that the children were thirteen and fifteen, the house could not contain their music, their friends, or their dreams of detachment. It appeared to each privately in turn that the stairs from the front door up to the bedroom floor shook and resounded all day and late into the night with pounding footsteps, and each in turn was struck with the amount of dirt carried in from the street. From the window of the tiny room used for sewing and laundry and only occasionally for guests, Alice could see the minster and the charming huddle of roofs around it, but even in October the air of the low-lying marshy city was cold and damp, and at night she shivered under her duvet from the draughts piercing the leaky window. There were difficulties too over the hot water, which had to climb too far from the basement furnace to stay warm enough for more than one bath at a time. Downstairs the whine of saws and polishers often interrupted the confidences of Gwen's patients, and the smell of glues and epoxies and lacquers floated up to nauseate them. Gwen's failure to complain was as good as a complaint in itself.

To balance his indebtedness to her, Billy made a habit of sighing over the spaciousness of privileged living that his wife had enjoyed in her early childhood. Useless to point out that Quondam Hall was even colder and dirtier; it was space, or rather the idea of space, that appealed to him. The Quondam Hall outbuildings, now mostly empty, provoked a reticence in him as penetrating as his wife's. Once, going round them with their children, Gwen heard him explaining the uses of each one. "This was the dairy, you see, Julian . . . here was the bakehouse, where the baking was done for the thirty or forty members of the household every weekday." And they would brush aside the cobwebs and peer into the huge ovens. "There the servants and officers hung the meat for the household, there they brewed the beer, here they did the laundry, washing the accumulated linen in huge vats two or three times a year and hanging it on lines overhead or draping it over bushes in the back garden. Your family and their dependents lived as if they were a village sufficient to itself, supplied by its home farm, its own flocks and herds, its own orchards, its own kitchen garden . . ." And the children would turn with bashful smiles, seeing only the decrepitude and dirt and feeling only the weight of the past. As soon as they could, they slipped out to play in the garden and wood and the little park beyond while their father mused upon the elaboration of the ancillary buildings and their mother waited for him, hard-faced, at the kitchen entrance.

The day after Alice had been to see Peter Wilson and heard of Esmé's plan to move to Akeld, Anthony himself called Gwen to make his offer of the hall. As she considered the offer, Gwen thought that at least her husband would be happy to live there. Somewhere among the outhouses he'd find himself the perfect site for a workshop. He was capable of an excellent job of rescue and restoration, and with luck he might get public money to carry it out, because the buildings were handsome and historically interesting and the local council was in the grip of conservation fever. As for the children, they would find themselves a ready-made music room, a library, a ballroom for bevies of friends, an attic stuffed with the discarded items of several centuries too good to throw away, not to speak of a huge garden, kitchen garden and orchard, all in the great embrace of Quondam Hall. It was less clear how Gwen herself would function there. She was sceptical about whether the move would work professionally, and wondered if the fine balance between her calling and her husband's wouldn't be upset. The move would have little point if she had to go to the expense of renting an office in the city. Would her town patients come out to the village and face the suffocating social patronage implied by its manor house? She thought not. It wouldn't matter in Holland or Denmark, where in spite of monarchies a republican spirit prevailed. What was different in the kingdom of Great Britain? More jewels, more ceremonial, more uniforms, more snobbery, more resentment, less assumption of equality before the law? Social privilege (if that's what it was) shouldn't matter here. She would insist on it not mattering, and see what happened. She called the head of social services at the county hospital and received assurances. It did not matter what sort of building you saw your patients in. To see them in a grand country house setting showed an up-to-date spirit. The clients should be pleased. "Anyway," the colleague noted coarsely, "it'll give your image a boost."

Gwen told this to her mother, who looked back at her with the long stare of objectivity. "Twit," said Alice, coming round from her revery. She was thinking about *image*. Both Gwen and Reggie were tall and thin and fair, with long legs, a pair of herons who would rise terrifyingly with white wings outstretched in languid slow motion. "Do you confront your patients?" she inquired. She was picturing Jess Wilson consulting Gwen.

"At times. If they demand confrontation. Most don't."

"I wouldn't. Would I be wrong?"

"There is no *wrong*," smiled Gwen. "You are too gentle to confront."

"Really?" Alice often felt like a raging bull. "I didn't tell you. I went to see a counsellor in New York—about Bob. She was a waste of time."

"Did you think of confronting her? She may have wanted that. We British sound glib to Americans, I'm afraid—we're so fluent, don't you agree?"

"I found I was more intelligent, not more glib. And she was nasty, for my own sake, apparently. 'Who do you think you are,' I said. 'I'm paying you to be kind to me.'"

Gwen smiled a tiny smile.

"Such cruelty!" continued her mother. "I wanted comfort. I wanted love, let me admit it: a loving kindly friend. What's wrong with that? What's wrong with comfort?" Gwen was silent, as she often was with her talkative patients. "Where do we stop fitting in?" Alice asked. "Where do we decide to disagree and must contradict? When I was a child, I was forbidden to contradict. But I encouraged you to do so. There are such disadvantages in not being able to contradict. If you just say nothing and walk away in a dignified fashion, people may not notice. Anthony never did. Bob Winship used to say, 'But why didn't you say something?' 'But I did,' I said; I said it by my behaviour. Your father never knew I was giving something up for him. He thought me frightfully selfish."

"Father is the most selfish man I know."

"Surely not as bad as that."

"There you go again, Mother."

Alice sighed. "I'll tell you this, Gwen: when I decided to leave your father, the decisiveness nearly killed me. I was not used to being decisive." She was joking; Gwen smiled. Alice wondered why children disapproved so heartily of their parents, particularly if the parents were virtuous, as she believed herself to be. No doubt because virtues were boring. And their boringness made her apologise for them. She should drop toleration, compassion, and so forth and be more dynamic; and indeed she was more dynamic in faraway New York. One is less dynamic with one's children than with others because one wishes to give room to the fledglings. Though Gwen was far from a fledgling. Indeed, Gwen frightened her a little: competent, professional Gwen. So Alice was not giving her room to develop so much as praising her as a mother should. She tried to shift the emphasis and succeeded in sounding patronising. "It's nice to see you and Billy getting on so well."

"We've worked things out. He's a good egg, Billy." Gwen brushed the patronage aside. She started talking about her father's offer of the hall and the estate. What did her mother think about it?

"Peter Wilson said yesterday that Esmé wanted my support, to persuade Anthony that a transfer would be a wise and clever thing to do. So she's succeeded already?"

"She's been talking about it for years, and I think Dad must have been coming round. He needed only a touch to get things rolling."

"Whose touch?"

"He took the credit on himself." They both laughed. "Oh, laughing is unkind of us," Gwen said with satisfaction. "I thought he was only pretending to be decisive, and therefore overdoing things, wanting to know how soon we'd be prepared to move in and take over, wanting to know how much I loved him . . ."

"Gracious." They couldn't help laughing again. Alice said judiciously, "One always wants to know how much one is loved, especially if one hopes one is loved a great deal. One cannot be told too often . . . though one learns not to ask. In point of fact, though, I realise that I no longer care how much I am loved."

"That is because you know how much."

"Oh, good gracious, I wasn't fishing for compliments. So what did you say to your father?"

"That I loved him madly, of course. What else could I say? Besides, it's true."

"Well, I'm very glad." Goodness, I am jealous, Alice thought. Anthony doesn't deserve to be loved as much as I do, considering how little he's done for the girls; but who gets his deserts? Better more than less. She saw what she had to say. "Gwen, don't let Anthony give up the hall. He needs it, and I think it would destroy you."

"Mother . . ."

"I mustn't interfere."

"That's right. We are adults."

"Esmé's age."

"Yes!"

"She is a sly puss, Esmé, isn't she?"

"I am a sly puss too, Mother."

"And Reggie. Reggie talks such rubbish, I don't know where I am with her. I am against this plot, Gwen. It will go to your heads and you'll go mad, both of you, with that huge house, and the estate, and your wilful father, and Esmé."

"Mother," said Gwen, with the air of one putting things straight, "do you remember leaving Father once, when Reggie and I were eight and nine or thereabouts? Two or three years before the final break. You hauled us out of the stables where we had been playing, and you made us have baths and put on our best clothes, and then you called Simmons to take us to York Station. 'We're going to London,' you told us. 'Go and say goodbye to your father.' 'Why, isn't Dad coming?' I said. 'Don't ask,' you said. 'Go and do as I say.'

"I began to get the wind up, but off I went, by myself, Reggie, of course, refusing to go, and I trotted through the hall looking for Dad here and there, until I found him on his knees weeding the lawn.

Weeding the lawn, my father, who never lifted a finger to do work he considered unbefitting! Very odd, I told myself, and went up and said, 'Dad, I've come to say goodbye.' But he didn't look up, he just went on weeding with a special sort of prong, heaving up dandelions and throwing them in a heap. 'Go along with her if you want,' he said at last, 'but don't expect me to say goodbye if you do.'

"Then I knew that you and he had quarrelled, and we were as good as dead, and I started to scream, wanting to stay with him even though he rejected me. I knew you'd arranged this perfectly dreadful situation for your own satisfaction. You were using me. You didn't give a damn for my feelings, I was only a child. 'Go along,' he said. I said, 'No, I want to stay.' He said, 'Go along, damn you!' Eventually I went, thinking I'd die of sorrow."

"What dreadful things we do to our children," Alice said, covering her eyes. "You didn't remind me of this before now."

"It wasn't relevant until now. Father fetched us back, didn't he? He came up to London and took us to a matinee and then we caught the train back to York. I never quite trusted you again. No explanation, just do as I say and you'll be all right. And it wasn't all right, it was agony!" Gwen's voice sounded out of control. "And then it was out again, you dragging us with you, not asking us what we wanted. We had no choice. We couldn't stay with the new young wife, the beauteous Esmé, we had to go with you, the discarded wife, as we thought, the disgraced and discarded old wife. Well, we'd rather have stayed with our father, on the winning side. In time we said to ourselves that we went out of loyalty to you, in so far as we considered our own consciences. We left the wonderful old house that we loved so much, Reggie and I, and the father we respected and loved. Listen, Mother: we found Father glamorous beyond words. He was amusing, he was distinguished, he was famous, and elegant."

"Gracious, Gwen. Dare I say that I can hardly believe you? You wouldn't give him the time of day. Wasn't I glamorous and distinguished enough for you? You certainly clung close enough to me. You were always saying how much you loved me. And of course I loved you. I thought I did all I should by you. I find you unbelievably hard."

"That's the way it seemed to me at the time, though I tried to explain it away because I understood that you really did love us. Over the years I've come to understand the situation a great deal more clearly. But don't you expect me to listen to your theories of right and wrong over our moving back into the hall. Don't pretend all of a sudden that you have Dad's welfare at heart. Ask yourself if you aren't envious of what you threw away."

"I cannot stay with you any longer if you go on like this. Your father was doing you a great deal of damage. What sort of damage?— not loving you; indulging himself; womanizing, gambling, shouting about suicide, and I took you away with me because I was afraid of leaving you behind with him." Alice met Gwen's eyes and held her anger. Gwen looked down.

They were sitting in Gwen's drawing-room on the first floor of the house overlooking a series of slate and pantile roofs descending to the Ouse. The holiday crowds that swarmed along the quays in warm summer weather had gone. The season was over. York was now a pleasant small city for its residents, who could walk and shop at last without being jostled by tourists. Alice had planned taking the Bowerses to a concert in a few days. It was to be a surprise; the children were musical. Now she felt punished and humiliated and in no fit state to inaugurate a family expedition calculated to please each member. How could any of them submit to her leadership? And yet she had brought up her daughters single-handedly, since Anthony took no notice of them and contributed very little to their upkeep. She had developed her business by working very long hours and studying business management, of which she'd known nothing. She'd been cheerful and encouraging to the girls all the while. She went to every concert, every play their school put on; she sat in on every conference, every prize-giving, every sports day and speech day, taking pains to find the right elegant, faintly dull clothes, and smiling as if bursting with approval and friendliness when in fact she wanted to lie down and sleep. Oh, enough: she'd done what all parents did, and she'd done it with rapture. And to be told now that it was their father whom they'd found heroic! The injustice of it was unspeakable.

It took a moment for Alice's common sense to reassert itself. Meanwhile, Gwen too had recovered. "Stay, Mother dear. I've had to live with these thoughts for years; surely you can live with them for a few days longer. Besides, where will you go? To Reggie's? She hasn't room. To a hotel? Mother dear, you might as well face the truth."

"Is it the truth, Gwen? Or is it revenge?"

"That's something you have to decide for yourself." Gwen now crossed the room with her heron stride and threw her arms round her mother and hugged her.

Alice suffered herself to be hugged, but she thought she could do without that affection, if affection it was.

"I can go to a hotel," she said mildly, thinking of how much more comfortable she'd be. But Gwen laughed.

The truth! The truth will set us free! There was always a point, Alice believed, when you look cruelty in the eye and decide whether or not to be cruel. She was conscious that more than once she had practised cruelty as an art form, having supposed living itself was an art. The trouble was that Gwen had always been competent, and her competence gave the .impression that she would survive any mishandling. Not for her the displays of temper and tears by which other children answered adversity. Gwen was calm, even placid, with an endearing rectitude. As a little girl she would sort her clothes at night and arrange clean ones for the morning without being told. She would stuff her shoes with paper before putting them away, so they kept their shape. She did her homework on time, and her little desk was kept immaculate, with neat stacks of paper, sharpened pencils, notebooks correctly labelled and constantly revised. She always knew the date and the time of day. She knew the principal rivers of the world and the annual income of the average Bangladeshi peasant. Now that she was near forty, she would never permit her mother to be put in an old people's home, but would keep her in her own place, well nourished, warm, though short of the booze and sex and trashy reading one disapproves of for the serious old but which they pine for.

Reggie, on the other hand, selfish and furtive herself, would not know anything about proper nutriments or the dangers of hypothermia, but would provide champagne and oysters, even as she borrowed (and lost) Alice's remaining jewels and finery, because they represented fun. Reggie could be as soft and doughy and spicy and sweet as a hot-cross bun, marked with its sugar cross, but she could be hard, too, as if she had the significances of the wooden cross and its nails always with her and only used her bun character as a folk version, to pop into the popular mouth. She had four daughters, all fair and blue eyed and as yet prettily angular. It was they whom she schemed for in an old-fashioned way, thinking of how much more advantageous for them to live in Quondam Hall than in their handsome suburban house in handsome suburban Harrogate.

Visiting her there, Alice discovered that Reggie's family put in a block vote for moving to the hall. Reggie's spouse, Jeremy Smith, worked for Sotheby's, and it would suit him to have Quondam Hall for his address. He would know a lot of its history and find out even more, correct Pevsner, write a leaflet, a book, a television programme on the hall and its builder and its owners. As for the girls, they could have the ponies they were always scheming for. In cooperation with Gwen and Delia, Reggie might put in some decent heating and an up-to-date kitchen and have the place painted properly. To pay for restoration and improvements, they might try and bring in properly guided groups of Americans, using Alice as a contact person in New York, charging £100 each for a detailed tour and a good dinner prepared in the new kitchen. Such an arrangement would be more in keeping with the character of the hall than the visitors Esmé had now—groups from the Women's Institutes at £3 a head. As for the estate, which included most of the village of Hartland, commercial rents could be tripled and ordinary house rents doubled and perhaps farm rents too. They were absurdly low at the moment, thanks to Anthony's negligence. He had always refused to use an agent. But the finances of the estate merited a professional advisor. Who would be the best person to hire? They would have to look about.

Alice listened to this Machiavellian talk in disbelief but admiration. Worldliness that she had acquired by sheer hard work and many mistakes her daughters had arrived at naturally in the course of growing up.

"Love you out of this world, Pa," Reggie duly said within Alice's hearing when Anthony telephoned about the possible move and sounded out Reggie's affection for him. "Love yer, Pa!"

This makeshift and spurious declaration appeared to be acceptable to the father. Alice, ex-wife, migrant and therefore irresponsible, even though sobered from Gwen's brutality, was ready to offer more trouble. They were seated in Reggie's prettily uncomfortable drawing-room. What Alice hated most was the good taste: the hard Georgian settees, lights too dim to read by, side tables too high for a glass or cup, frightful swagged curtains. "Reggie, you know how I feel about your father's move to give you the hall?"

"Lay off, Mum. Mummy should go back to Bobby in Um-murrica."

"His name is Robert Winship. Don't talk to me like that, I can't bear it."

"Now, Mummy, why shouldn't we take up our birthright? You cheated us out of it, after all, right?"

"Not right!" Alice was ready to cry.

"If you'd stuck with Dad, we'd all be better off now."

So unkind, Alice thought, appalled and distressed to the point that she wondered if she shouldn't warn Anthony—and even Esmé also—of Reggie's ruthlessness. But perhaps they knew? And Alice said to her daughter, "Reggie, I left your father in order that he might try to beget a son with another wife. That's not the only reason, but it was one of the chief reasons."

"What's that to do with me? And if you're talking about Esmé, I can't say that she tried very hard to conceive a son. One daughter, that's all—I don't call that trying. I had four daughters, myself, before we gave up."

"Four darling girls, four pearls," her mother offered. She was deeply fond of her grandchildren. It seemed to her that they had sweet ways and gentle confiding manners. "I know Jeremy and you wanted a boy. However, Anthony's case involves a direct male heir for an ancient estate. You know that. It's not quite the same thing as simply wanting a boy. And then, I think she would have gone on trying for one if other things had been right."

"Oh, you mean Dad's gambling and screwing. That's nothing."

"On the contrary, Reggie. I think it meant a lot to Esmé."

Reggie laughed. "A lot you know about it, Ma."

And Alice, hurt and angry, said that she knew a fair amount. Reggie stared and said, "Do you think Delia is Dad's child?" Then she too looked hurt and angry and actually blushed.

"Whose, then, if not Anthony's?" Alice mustered her calmest reflections.

"What does it matter? In fact it doesn't matter. She's a girl, not a boy to carry on the grand succession of Quondams. Anyway, Dad adores her, that is what matters. Unfair to Gwen and me though it is. That's what I blame you for."

"Blame me for?"

"Unfair, isn't it?—to be blamed for something that happened in spite of your good intentions."

"It is time, I think, that you grew up and forgave your mother," said Alice bravely. "I forgave mine, and she forgave hers. It is time for you to forgive me."

"Oh—forgive!" sneered Reggie. "If forgiveness is all you want, that's easy: I forgive you."

It was the same old story. Alice could not be bothered to become further upset. It was a relief to leave and drive back to York, choosing lovely byways and pretty villages where little had changed since she was mistress of Quondam Hall. As she drove, she reverted to Peter Wilson's admission that he had felt passion for Esmé at one time. If Delia was Peter's, Anthony had no reason to favour her. Perhaps it did not do to look too closely at ancestry. Delia was lovely and everyone loved her. Alice took comfort in that and thought that Reggie and Gwen should do the same even if they weren't Delia's half sisters as it was thought they were. Only Reggie's accusation of unfairness rankled.

So the hall was to be theirs, as they once took for granted. It was a reward for being who they were. It was also to be an expiation for the sin of whatever had caused their expulsion from Eden. They might even begin to think of Alice more kindly once they were in place in the hall. And yet, was it theirs, to be accepted just because Anthony suddenly wanted to give it to them?

Anthony Quondam hurried along the gravel path from the garden front of his big old house to the stable block, with the slightly hectic, slightly effeminate trot of an old man. His shanks had lost some muscle and his pelvis had broadened. His spine had lost its arch and begun to curve forward, a tendency he fought by habitually throwing his chest out. He carried his large silvery head askew to balance a shoulder that was now carried lower than the other one. His bright dark eyes stared out enthusiastically from under his black hairy brows and the wild mane of white hair that he kept stroking back with one hand. He had decided to let his beard grow, and it was coming out as white as the hair on his head but bushier, and he was not sure whether to keep it or shave it off. He would ask Delia whether she liked it.

He liked Delia. She continually astonished him as his other daughters failed to do. He thought often how beautiful and talented she was, and how she was yet his daughter. Alone he had begot her, bred her, loved her. Now he was going to reward inscrutable fate by giving her the best part of his house. He couldn't wait to tell her. He knew he would find her in the studio he had set up for her after she'd gone down from university. The barn she inhabited opened off the old kennel yard and was oak and stone, solid, with a good dry floor. In its airy sweet-smelling space, Anthony had installed an immense cast-iron stove that had once warmed the waiting room of York Station. He had also doubled-glazed the slits that provided air and light and put in skylights of Perspex on the northern side. There was a double door to keep out the cold and wet. The space was now quiet and warm, and its light was a pure Arctic light, devoid of yellow, that brought out detail without casting much shadow. As he entered it, Delia appeared in startling focus wearing a plain white shirt and dark cotton trousers in the heart of a black and white photograph. She had put her current canvases face to the wall and was simply standing, contemplating, pencil or pen or charcoal stick in hand, before an easel to which she had pinned a large sheet of paper. There was a large elaborate drawing on it, apparently of figures in a landscape. He closed the door and stood before her, panting. If the other dear girls had spoken of their love for him in a fine exaggerated way, shouldn't Delia outdo them, since he loved her fifty times more than he loved them?

"Delia, I had to see you."

She came forward smiling and pulled a kitchen chair from a wreckage of canvases and frames in a corner.

"You need a comfortable chair in here," he said. "Or two chairs. Why don't you ask for them?"

"I'm all right!"

"Of course you're 'all right,' but it's not very comfortable for you, darling. I want you to have everything you feel you need."

"It's perfectly comfortable, Dad"—and waited, still with a slight, delighted smile.

"That's so wonderful!"—jerking his head at the drawing. She immediately picked a white cloth off the back of the easel and covered the paper. "Sorry, I shouldn't . . ."

"It's just that . . ."

"Don't explain. You like to keep it unseen until you've finished it." She nodded, not an inch more than was necessary.

"All your work, it seems to me, is *wonderful*."

She shook her head and went red. At the same time her eyes unexpectedly welled with tears.

He was astounded. "Ah, Delia! What have I said to disturb you? And I had such good things to tell you!" He was terribly upset at her tears. They fell in silence, running down her cheeks and wetting her white shirt with long smears, and she made no move to mop them or stop them. "What's wrong, can't I praise your work?"

"No." Her voice was perfectly clear.

"Don't you love me, Delia, my darling child?"

"Of course."

"Can't a father delight in his daughter's work?"

"I haven't done anything delightful. Your delight has nothing to do with me." She threw the cloth back, ripped the paper off the easel and tore it in half and those halves again in half and threw the shreds on the floor. Then she dried her eyes with the handkerchief he offered her and stood staring at him, clearly wishing him to go. "What have you come to see me about?"

But the rapture of his generosity had passed and he felt an outsider on his own property, humiliated by a girl sixty years younger than he was, flesh of his flesh, blood of his blood, who wished him dead. Nevertheless he went on with what he had to say. He could not just turn and go. He could not find a more congenial moment to speak than this one. Even now, when she heard what he had to say, she might relent, she might throw her arms round his neck. It was not impossible. She had often thrown her arms round his neck when she was a little child. A more adorable child it was hard to imagine. Now, a grown woman, she might come to the point of apologising. Apology cost nothing. It was a gesture, nothing more. She could surely afford a little gesture towards her father. His voice became unnaturally syrupy. "I came to tell you that your mother and I are leaving the hall and going to live in Akeld as soon as it can be fixed up. We're splitting the hall and the estate into three parts, one for you, one for Gwen, one for Reggie."

He waited. He even thought she might cry again, this time out of love and gratitude. If she did, he would embrace her wholeheartedly, understanding that she had to balance her mysterious resentment with a clear and candid receptivity. He said to her fondly, "Nothing is guaranteed to us, Delia." He meant to imply that fate is paramount.

She said, "I don't want any part of it."

"Alice ran away, with your sisters, to survive, I honestly believe. But you know, Delia, I found them boring, your sisters. So narrow, so pious in some piety I didn't recognise. Do you know what I'm saying, darling? I haven't threatened you, have I? You know what: a tree, to flourish, must have its roots in the mud. My roots are in the mud, I think. Oh, I am sorry to be so old. So difficult for you. I had a past, Delia. You can't have dreamed of it. It's of no consequence to you now, I understand that clearly. I don't prize it myself. But it is there, if you have need of it. If you ever have to take me seriously." She fidgeted and said nothing, and kept her eyes on the floor in front of her. After a moment, he heard himself pleading. "I thought you'd be glad of my present. Why are you behaving in this churlish fashion? I'll give you the staterooms and the stable block, with the rose garden and the orchard and the dovecot. You'll be independent. You'll have a special fund put aside specially to convert it into your very own house, exactly the way you want it."

"But I don't want it." She spoke in a low, clear voice as if she had been rehearsing with a master. "Believe me, you're very kind, but I'm happy as I am. Thank you. Don't think I don't love you. I honour you in everything you do."

Anthony stared at her bitterly. "So, thank you very much. You can't stay here, you know, after we've gone. We're giving the place to your sisters too, so if you don't want your part of the hall and the stable block, you can leave."

"If you want me to leave, I shall do so. I won't stay with Reggie and Gwen. I know them."

"You can go and live in a damned caravan in a caravan park and see how you like that," he shouted.

"If you wish it."

"And don't think you'll get a pretty cottage or anything like that, because there aren't any. I've sold as many as I couldn't rent and I can't afford to do more." The blood gathered behind his eyes, squeezing them forward, and a sliver of pain crept along a crevice in his forehead just above his left eye.

"I don't want you to do more." Her voice became soft, as if she were tired. Even Gwen and Reggie had more bounce in their voices when he telephoned them, and of course they had said, each in her way, that they were immensely fond of him. He couldn't think what had got into this one, whom he'd been mistaken in believing the best of the lot.

"The sooner you go the better, then. We're moving to Akeld. Did you think perhaps you were getting Akeld? It was you who told me the Amorys were leaving. So we're having it done up." He staggered to his feet, kicking over the kitchen chair. "Not a kiss? Nothing? To hell with you then." He got to the door somehow.

"Wait," said Delia.

He stood shaking at the door. "Yes?"

She spoke painfully. "You're giving away everything? For nothing?"

"*What?*"

"Giving it away for nothing?"

"For nothing. For love." The phrase pleased him.

"But it's yours. You can't give it away."

"What rubbish! I can give it away exactly because it's mine."

Her painfulness increased. "Even if you gave it away, it would still be yours. That's how I see it. I can't take what is yours."

"Nothing shall come of nothing!"

"Let *them* say what you want to hear."

"They will! They do!" He waited another second before flinging open the door and rushing out, but she showed no expression.

3

Esmé would have been relieved to hear herself called a sly puss. She thought of herself in far worse terms. The trouble was that the deceits she practised were part of a great network of thought which covered her like camouflage. She had begun to be underhanded quite young, when she despaired of getting her own way. She was absurdly inarticulate in those days, and believed herself to be friendless, so there wasn't much to lose. Underhanded people didn't need eloquence or allies. Of course her schemes could rebound and crush her, but she was often crushed anyway. In fact there were advantages in appearing crushable. She used to wheedle Anthony shamefully when she was playing the child bride to the master of Quondam Hall, that famous public man. Now that she was forty-four, the weakness was no more than an absurd mask, and to be a sly puss was to be clever, if in an unpleasant way. She would have been glad to be called a subtle, traditional woman with a taste for intrigue. She had certainly intrigued to make Anthony believe that he wanted to move to Akeld.

In being this traditional woman, Esmé thought that her guile had been created and regulated by her past. She explained it to herself by her mother's death in childbirth when Esmé was twelve. If her mother hadn't died then, she might have learned to get her own way as sweetly as her mother did, voice never raised, with a direct look at whom she was addressing and a disarming smile later. People seemed to remember that Esmé was once spontaneous, but certainly after the mother's death there was a change and Esmé looked down and was silent or spoke so as to suggest that she agreed or had no opinion. Her character disappeared underground like a rabbit. Her disagreements, reported back, came as a surprise: "Esmé doesn't think so," or "Esmé doesn't care for that"—but she seldom said so directly.

After the funeral, Esmé spoke of her mother's death only twice, once to Anthony Quondam on her wedding night and once to Peter Wilson when life with Anthony struck her as hard. Yet it was an event that Esmé didn't get over. If she didn't talk about it, or even think of it much, that was not owing to a deliberate decision; it happened more like a fault, or a short in an electrical system that leaves an area blank. She had to learn to talk of it as stroke victims learn speech again, and she never quite mastered it.

The birth had taken place at home, in accordance with Mrs. McEachnie's wishes after a badly managed delivery of her first baby in hospital. The deliveries at home had been easy, and six children ran about the place—the eldest, born in hospital, and five born at home of whom Esmé was the first. The house was warm and comfortable and spacious; a midwife was in charge, a special nurse in attendance, and a beloved and trustworthy family doctor on call, a man whose mumbled boast was, with pathetic irony, that he'd delivered over three thousand babies and never lost a mother.

On this last occasion all had gone equally well, and a beautiful strong baby boy lay in the McEachnie cradle. Esmé and her next sister went up to see him and their mother as soon as the smiling doctor had driven off. They were on the point of entering the bedroom when they heard the nurse on the telephone calling for the doctor to be summoned back as soon as he reached his surgery, and running footsteps in the bedroom, and frantic calls for ice from the housekeeper. The girls went in and their first impression was of the bright red sheets on the bed. Their mother was laid flat, the pillows that should have been under her head now elevating her hips, and all the bedclothes and her night dress shining with that bright red blood that comes straight from the heart. From the post-partum hemorrhage Mrs. McEachnie died very quickly. There was nothing to be done. The doctor arrived back full tilt from his surgery in minutes, but, poor man, without the means for a blood transfusion, he was useless. Like the midwife and the nurse, he wobbled and was pale, as if underwater. She was taken, he said. Mrs. McEachnie walked with God, and God took her. You must be brave. Think of the others. Think of the newborn, so utterly on his own now, poor mite, to be fed on other women's milk, expressed in the hospital and hurried over to the joyless nursery. Think of the father, astounded in his industrialism, for whom things had always prospered until now, standing at his windows overlooking the river and thinking of Job.

Esmé refused this pious nonsense. "Why not think of me?" she asked the doctor. "I loved her more than anyone. I was the apple of her eye. She loved giving birth to me here in our house. My birth was easy and she loved me for it. I was the first one to be born at home, do you remember? But I misled her, didn't I? If she'd had her babies in the hospital, she wouldn't be dead now."

"Wheest," said the doctor, in that peculiarly Scottish demand for silence and good sense, and he eyed her with horror.

Esmé went back to boarding school like a good girl, mindful of all that was expected of her and of her own incapacity to do anything of the sort. She felt frozen. She could love nothing and no one—God, country, her father, her brothers and sisters, her friends. Years later, Peter Wilson asked kindly of her, as his friend Anthony's very young new wife, "What do you miss, here in Yorkshire, out of all you have at home in Borders?"

Esmé smiled at him shyly and answered in her oblique way that the only thing she missed was what she had missed for the last six solid years—her Siamese kitten and its friend her big buck rabbit. The two of them played together hilariously like clowns in a circus. Esmé had given them to her small brother when their mother died. "And you still miss them?" Peter Wilson asked incredulously.

"Yes. Isn't that silly? Do you know why I gave them away? Because they didn't take any notice of me. Not enough notice, anyway. They didn't care, OK? Do you know that I actually thought of killing them? Do you understand what I'm saying?"

Barely. Or no. What a weird girl. She didn't miss her family—she missed a kitten and a rabbit that must be dead now anyway, in the ordinary course of nature. Apart from those animals, nothing touched her, Esmé related, and she would never miss anyone or anything again. Mourning for her mother jammed her like seawater in a watch. Of course she must be lying. A melodramatic girl, an embarrassing girl. Pretty, though. Radiant.

"But you feel for Anthony?"

"Oh, of course. Of course. What a funny thing to say. That was six years ago. Everything's different now."

Peter Wilson took these sentences home and pondered them in his heart. And eventually Esmé came to him and told him the rest, as he'd known she would.

Two years after her mother's death her father married again, as much for his children's sake as for his own. The stepmother was a vigorous fair-haired woman, a neighbour, a widow in her thirties. The McEachnie children had already picked her out as a likely replacement for their mother. She had very soon swooped down on them after the funeral and sorted them out and got the household ticking over nicely again, and been tactful with the eldest and calming with the little ones. Only Esmé baulked at enthusiasm. She became evasive at home, flirtatious abroad, a miserably thin high-spirited girl, totally wrong about herself. At length the family doctor put her in hospital, where she regained weight and began to understand the distortion she was offering herself. Her family used to have a cottage on the low moors near the Whiteadder on the Border, and it was near there, when she was seventeen, that she met Anthony Quondam, who was fishing for trout as he did every year. She watched him from the cover of birch and fir where the river rushes into gorges. She saw a dark, handsome man with black and grey hair, tall and kingly. All the McEachnie children fished, and Esmé saw that Anthony knew his business. She came back to see him the next day and the next. Eventually he noticed her and started talking to her.

Peter Wilson could see why. A few months at Hartland and she was filling out, her face getting plumper and red-cheeked while her body stayed as slender as a gymnast's, but Peter could see how waiflike she must have been. When she mused, her copper-coloured hair framed the pale freckled skin in a way that made Peter think of Bellini Virgins with babies in rocks where a river ran much like the Whiteadder.

"Anthony found me amusing, I think," she said. "Then he could not take his eyes off me. Isn't that idiotic?"

She managed to run into Anthony again at the fishers' inn at Ellemford and invited him to fish near the McEachnie cottage. The father turned up at the inn to sort things out and discovered that he knew Anthony Quondam already. They'd both been in the army of North Africa during the war, Quondam a brigadier, McEachnie a major in Special Services, carrying out lightning strikes behind enemy lines with fast lightly armed vehicles. "They liked each other," Esmé said. "Their campaigns gave them a lot in common. Anthony came to supper twice. Our cottage is nice. It's a nice long way from Hartland, too. It was quite difficult for him at home. He minded that Gwen and Reggie went quiet when he appeared. He said Alice was clever, but he didn't seem glad, just that she could take care of herself, because they were in the middle of the divorce. It was kind of nice for Anthony that Pa and the boys made dirty jokes all the time, and my stepmother and my sisters gave as good as they got."

"Did you too?" Peter asked.

"No, I didn't. I was never very good at repartee. I enjoyed it, mind you, but I was never a laughy-laughy, have-at-you kind of person, and they all knew that, so it was all right."

The father and Anthony joked over Esmé's invitation to fish nearby. "Little twat!" McEachnie declared, not unlovingly, but Esmé overheard him and the ensuing hoot of laughter from them both. She longed to humiliate them in return. "I had my pride too," she told Peter Wilson. She heard Anthony pressed to go fishing in a famous pool. He said he'd be there before breakfast, and she slipped out of the house before dawn, throwing her father's quilted tweed shooting jacket over her nightie. When Anthony waded into the stream off the bank he found her in the deepest part swimming. She pulled herself out and faced him, wringing out her hair.

"*You* faced Anthony stark naked in the river?" Peter Wilson interrupted at this point.

Esmé laughed. "Who else?"

"It's hard to believe."

"I don't care whether you believe me or not, Peter, that's what happened. Why should I lie to you? I'm not particularly proud of what I did. I'm more surprised, when I look back. But you know, in our family, no one took much notice of nakedness. In the cottage we walked about bare all the time. It didn't mean anything to us. At school the girls said that once men see you naked, they had to have you, which I thought was hilarious, so it was a way of getting back at Anthony and Pa. I mean . . ."

"I know what you mean," Peter Wilson said. "All too clearly."

"You're shocked!" Esmé said, amused. "Shall I tell you what happened next?" By the following year she considered herself grown up and had run off a couple of times from Kelso, where their big house was. She'd take the bus to Edinburgh without saying when she'd return. Her brothers and sisters were critical. They thought that rejection of the stepmother was the trouble, not rejection of life. They had their futures worked out. They were going to universities and colleges and training institutions. They were going to be doctors and lawyers and chemists and zoologists. Esmé wasn't going to be anything much more than a flower child, they said, pointing out that the days of flower children were over. Next on the cards, they said, were street drugs. "My stepmother thought I was using drugs already. When I said I wasn't, she said that druggies were liars. So, I thought, that gives me plenty of scope to lie, because she doesn't believe me anyway. She found some packets of sugar in one of my drawers—the sort you get in a tea-room to put in your cup of tea. She insisted on burning them in case they were, you know, the other white stuff. I couldn't tell her that all you have to do to find out what it is, is to taste it. That would have given me away, right? It was all very silly."

"And a bit hysterical on her part," Peter observed.

"Right. The next thing that happened was that Anthony came to the Whiteadder again in April when the weather softened. The winds begin to blow softly from the Lammermuirs instead off the North Sea. The river pools are surrounded with the leafing rowans and birches and oaks. It is lovely, and it got to Anthony. He was pretty lonely. And then he admired my brothers, you know. He wished he had sons like them; he told me so. Oh, no, you're wrong, I said, you don't want boys like that in your house. He was amused. He liked the idea of Quondam Hall being full of dreadful boys shouting and swearing and tracking mud on the carpets and leaving their rods and guns all over the place."

Peter Wilson thought: also, Esmé would bring half a million

pounds with her. Anthony had told him, unashamed. The Quondams had a habit of marrying heiresses. Anthony's own mother brought money from coal mines, plenty of money when she married in 1910, less in the disastrous twenties and thirties, but enough for his mother and him to live on after his father had been killed on the Somme. During his minority the estate had brought negligible profit, agriculture up to the Second World War barely paying a livelihood. The mother's money had been indispensable.

If Alice had brought a fortune to her marriage, it might have saved it, Peter could see that now. In fact she brought remarkably little, Anthony grumbled. Her people had a big well-run and prosperous farm in Norfolk, but the idea that she should have a dowry or even much of an inheritance never occurred to them. Alice was brought up to earn her own living, and she was perfectly capable of doing so. Anthony even caught the suspicion that they thought Alice was marrying down. Yet she wasn't the usual "right sort of girl," according to Anthony. His mother, who liked her, said to Anthony, who repeated her words to his friend Peter: "You know what I mean, Anthony. She's marvellous, isn't she, but she knows nothing about people like us."

Peter wondered if Esmé was the right sort of girl either. What sort of girl was Esmé? She was fey, sensational.

"That second time Anthony came fishing, I was cold toward him," Esmé told him. "When he came forward to kiss me, I turned my head aside. 'Can't I have a kiss, Esmé?' he said. He looked crushed. I didn't care."

"You thought you had him in your pocket?"

"No, I just didn't care. It was as simple as that. While he was staying with us, on the Saturday, I slipped off to stay with a friend in Edinburgh who was throwing a gigantic party. The next morning, after church, they discovered I was missing. Good God, you'd think the world had come to an end." The stepmother informed Anthony that Esmé had slipped off "to look after a sick friend who'd called for help." "Frankly, I don't believe it," Mrs. McEachnie said, showing Esmé's note, written in careless scribbles and stating that she did not know when she'd be back. She'd added the friend's address and telephone number, probably as a sop.

"Why not believe her?"

Esmé was only eighteen. And then the stepmother confessed. "To tell the truth, Anthony, I'm mortally afraid of what she's up to. I rang at nine o'clock this morning to see how things were and she sounded drunk. But she doesn't drink. The funniest voice, slurring her words. Not like her. You know what a clear precise way of speaking she has."

"Go after her, then."

"Not I, Anthony. I'm half the trouble. Not her father. He's the other half of the trouble. It would have to be one of the boys, and I don't know whether they could manage it."

"I'll go with him."

"No, no. Why should you trouble? I'll send Rory."

But Rory, who was only sixteen, said she would take no notice of him, and Anthony offered again. "We'll both go. We'll bring her back."

"Are you sure you want to?" Rory asked.

"I knew she'd come with me," Anthony told Peter Wilson. "I thought of soldiers I'd brought back from the verge of suicide."

"Suicide?" Peter questioned. "Was there a question of suicide where Esmé was concerned?"

"I thought she was pretty desperate, tell the truth. She so plainly didn't give a damn about anything."

They're a good pair, Peter decided; both as melodramatic as they come.

Mrs. McEachnie called Esmé again. This time she replied only after a long interval and still in the same slurred manner. Mrs. McEachnie asked after the sick friend.

"Who?" After a long pause, the girl added, "Up all night. Don't ring again."

"I left for Edinburgh immediately," Anthony declared, in the manner of Caesar reporting a campaign. Young Rory acted as guide. He must have liked the red Mercedes, Peter thought, and of course Anthony drove it like a charioteer. The address Esmé had left on her message was in Dundas Street in the New Town, and could scarcely have been more respectable. The fourth-floor flat was said to belong to a school-teacher who rented a room to Esmé's friend Jane, the one who was supposed to be ill. It being Easter Day, there was no one about on the street, and for a long time no one answered the doorbell. After repeated pounding and cries by Rory through the letter box, Esmé herself opened the door, barefoot, wearing a man's filthy blue-and-white-striped shirt and wrinkling her forehead and blinking, trying to focus. "Completely spaced out," Rory said in disgust, as Anthony forced his way in by seizing her and carrying her before him into the flat. No one else was there. The flat was choked with litter, bedclothes, strewn clothing, dirty dishes. It smelled of burnt string, which was cannabis, and dirt, the dirt of sweat and unwashed clothes and sheets and decaying food on the kitchen counters and spilling out of the bin. There was a hypodermic on the bathroom wash-basin that Anthony picked up in his handkerchief and wrapped in plastic to take away as evidence if there was further trouble. Esmé didn't get more wakeful, so Anthony wrapped her in a blanket from one of the beds and they carried her down to the car. Returning to the flat in order to telephone the McEachnies, Anthony ran into a young man who came up the stairs behind him and inquired after Esmé.

"I asked him if he'd been there the previous evening," Anthony said.

The young man said that he had.

Then Anthony, according to his own account, put a hand to the young man's throat and shoved him back to the wall and shouted that if he was responsible for her condition, he'd better not come round there again or Anthony would break his legs! The moment he let go, the young man hared down the shallow stone steps and out the front door, round the corner, past Rory and his unconscious sister in the back of the Mercedes, and out of sight. "I'll kill you!" Anthony bellowed after him.

"But what condition was it that she was in?" Peter Wilson asked, puzzled by Anthony's heroic legend and feeling extremely prosaic and disbelieving.

"I'm not going to put a name to it," said Anthony. "As far as I'm concerned, the episode never took place. As I said to Rory, 'Don't breathe a word about this to anyone, ever. We have to consider her future.'"

"He was concerned about your future," Peter said to Esmé on that later occasion.

She laughed. "What future was that?"

"Your future with him? Tell me, what was wrong with you when he rescued you?"

"I was drunk," Esmé said.

As Peter Wilson pieced it together, Anthony told Mr. and Mrs. McEachnie in the evening that they were right to worry about her. They were home in front of a fire. Esmé was in her room upstairs. "But she's a grand girl. She needs taking care of, that's all. I'd marry her if I weren't so old."

"Are you old?" Mrs. McEachnie wrinkled her eyebrows. "I hadn't noticed." She was looking at him as if she had never thought about his age until then, and was assessing it rationally for the first time. What was he—forty? fifty? In any case, far too old for Esmé.

But vigorous, surely? With a stride people had to run to keep up with? And didn't life crackle under his feet? He said grandly, "I want to marry your daughter."

The father and stepmother heard in disbelief. "She does need a steadying hand, it's true," said Mrs. McEachnie out of courtesy.

"I have to know, because I'm on the Bench: is she an addict? She'd taken heroin, I think."

"No!" The McEachnies were appalled. "She hasn't the money to buy heroin!"

"You can easily find money if you want it badly enough," said the eldest sister with a touch of coarse realism. "You can steal it. Girls go whoring. No, wait. The fellow on the stairs that Anthony met—he was probably a pusher. He'd give her a few fixes, then later she'd have to pay." Her knowledge humiliated them. They had seen nothing.

The father suddenly came to his senses. "Anthony, it's your age, man. She's just a young girl. There'd be over thirty years between you. It's unheard of."

Anthony began to recite some lines dear to his mother:

"O is there no frowning of these wrinkled, ranked wrinkles deep,
Down? no waving off of these most mournful messengers,
still messengers, sad and stealing messengers of grey?
No there's none, there's none, O no there's none . . ."

43

He was quiet. They were electrified. They only half understood the words, only half understood what he was getting at. Their mouths hung open and then eased into smiles of astonishment. They looked at each other and took deep breaths. He added, "We may have many years together. She will live in comfort and safety with me. I will leave her well looked after. Then she will marry again. Of course she will marry again. Now: I'm a free man. My divorce has gone through. I can give her a fine home and a good name and a great estate. And sons and daughters."

Madness! "Have you spoken to her?" asked McEachnie, still sounding the rational line.

"She will say yes. I'd like to stay over tomorrow."

"Of course you will stay," said the father. "But there's to be no more talk of marriage."

"You must tell me if I may ask her to marry me. Sleep on it. If you say yes, I'll ask her before I go."

"I can't approve, because of your age," said the father, and added, with a weakness Peter Wilson fully understood, "But she's reached her majority. Ask her if you want."

Peter Wilson wondered if Anthony had ever in fact got round to saying how old he was. Of course, the McEachnies might have looked him up in *Burke's Landed Gentry* or *Who's Who*. Were the parents desperate, to permit him to propose to her? That's what Esmé had suggested when she told Peter how she'd ensnared Anthony. So was *she* desperate? Did she long to get away from home, or was she trying to act the part of the much-missed mother in a home of her own? The brothers must have made jokes, rough jokes about monkeys and goats, before they learned to shut up. It couldn't have been easy for Esmé to put up with them.

Once Esmé was in place, the marriage didn't seem as ridiculous as it might have been. A lot of men married very young girls. Established actors married starlets, full professors married students, sometimes one after the other as the wives aged. Peter Wilson had heard of such things. He was also told of distinguished women who married men twenty or thirty years younger than themselves. A modern phenomenon, something to recognise with a grin when you came across it. These were unconventional times; there were new arguments citing women's greater longevity and enhanced sexual function and their biological superiority to the male. But when all was said and done, the marriage remained the rough data of village gossip, never transmuted through the intelligence into coin of the realm.

But every time they went over these data, it was what they thought of as Esmé's passivity that people returned to with wonderment. It wasn't quite right in so young a person. So when she expressed—however deviously—a point of view, or a contrariness, they tended to nod and be pleased and to admire her for at last showing some spirit. Peter noticed that as Anthony's passion for her waned, he ceased to take her seriously, because of her seeming contradictions. Anthony would say as an excuse for his weakness, "So long as she's happy . . ." and Peter was horrified at the lack of understanding.

Some people to begin with, like Peter himself, rushed forward to help her with her weird enclosed system of contraries by firmly espousing certain personal truths—that she wasn't fat, or stupid, or denied. "You are yourself," he said to her. "You are really marvellous, you know that? Lovely, intelligent, charming Esmé!" Naïvely he told his wife, Jess, what Esmé and Anthony had told him separately of the strange wooing, and together Jess and he discussed the girl and her marriage. Gradually, Jess realised how jealous Peter was. She had been passively watching him being sucked into the confusion. Abruptly she put a stop to his enthusiasm. What in the world was Peter doing? Anthony meant more to them than Esmé. He was a public figure, a man who'd been a distinguished soldier and Member of Parliament, a thinking man, a superb friend, as opposed to a rather silly, pouting, worthless girl!

"What? All people have their own value? Well, to God, of course. But we're not God, are we," said Jess, who was a hard-thinking, efficient woman, a county councillor. "We have to think of their value to society, and Esmé doesn't amount to much, does she? You can't believe she's worth more than Anthony! You must be pulling my leg!" She also said, less controversially, that marriage to Esmé was Anthony Quondam's last chance of happiness, and no one, least of all his best friend, should try and tidy up his young wife by making her logical.

Peter was very much annoyed at his wife's insinuations, verging as they did on suspicion of his infidelity but not quite toppling over into accusation. He was mightily irritated at her Machiavellian comparison of human ways with God's. One should always act, he thought, with the highest possible motives. But when he chewed over the phrase "Anthony Quondam's last chance," he thought she was right, and backed off. Doesn't secondary advice often have such unexpected success? If you've got to do something, and don't want to do the chief thing you're urged to do, you can do the next best thing your advisors recommend, and they will be appeased.

Esmé took Peter Wilson's desertion as she took his infatuation, apparently with equanimity, but she went to her doctor and said she wanted to abort Anthony's baby that she was carrying, and in the ensuing uproar both Wilsons were appalled at what they had done to the young woman, so friendless, so alone, that she should seek to do such a thing. "Go and speak to her, Peter," said Jess with tears in her eyes. "I'd go myself, but I'm not supposed to know what you told me, am I? She might feel betrayed if she knew. So you go, and comfort her. We have to be very kind to that one."

Not that Jess wasn't terribly upset as she saw Peter hasten off to do his duty—crying like a madwoman at an upstairs window, as she later told Gwen in a counselling session, believing she'd sent him off to be unfaithful to her. But at least Esmé came to understand that she had what any girl might want—a great house, a great estate, a famous name, a lion of a husband, and then a baby to complete the picture. If she struck out for herself secretly, it was because she wasn't *any* girl, and told herself she didn't really want houses, estates, or lion husbands; but that was later, and by then she had Delia, the beloved.

What did she want, then? This was more obscure. She laughed at her worldly success, and got people to laugh with her. Secretly, though, she took everything too seriously. At first people were pleased and guessed that she wanted to be one of them. They were therefore very kind and hospitable to her. Then those selfsame people realised that she really was different: she was weird. More than that, she began to treat them as a toy might, in a smiley, mechanical way, and they began to feel as if they were being manipulated. For bit by bit Esmé found she could liven things up by putting ideas into people's heads.

For example: For years she complained to her neighbours and friends (who were chiefly Anthony's friends) about the dinginess and chill and inconvenience of the hall. That was nothing new. Alice had spoken in the same way. But Esmé got to the point of saying that the hall was unmanageable and always had been. Someone told her that Castle Howard had been so well constructed that, vast as it appeared— "twenty-seven bays and a dome"—three maids and a footman were all the staff it required to be kept clean and sweet. And it was as warm as an oven. That was in the early eighteenth century, before vacuum cleaners and central heating, she explained. No such luck with Quondam Hall. An amateur's job it was, no Hawksmoor to pick up the ideas and work them out in workmen's specifics; besides, it was much added to and full of quirks. At first Esmé was in a fright. Her mother and stepmother ran a spotless home. When the stepmother first took charge of the McEachnie household, she had said repeatedly, "That poor soul was a paragon!"—meaning Esmé's dead mother. So all was orderly and continued to be so. Everything worked, and went on working. Delicious wholesome meals turned up on the table every day, the larder was well stocked, there was always lots of hot water for baths and showers, the rooms were warm and airy, the household linen fresh, the towels vast and fluffy, just as before.

Strict control at Quondam Hall on the other hand had passed into the hands of untrained housekeepers who were sacked one after the other by Anthony after Alice's departure. Esmé inherited a mess she had no idea how to deal with. She would tackle one room—her bedroom was the first—and run instantly into intractable difficulties. The new central heating made the linenfold panelling shrink from the walls. New plumbing brought ghastly smells that couldn't be tracked down without digging up the lawns and the installing of baffles. Discreet double glazing put in at enormous cost caused such condensation that the windows wept all day. Anthony sometimes found his child bride weeping in dark corners. Then professionals would be summoned, architects, interior designers, builders, workmen. Gradually certain rooms became habitable, with the expenditure of vast amounts of Esmé's money and the capable advice of the stepmother from Kelso.

Then the trouble was that Esmé couldn't settle a good housekeeping regime in place. Get a capable housekeeper to take over and she abandoned her—escaped into the garden, into the park, to see friends, to London, to Edinburgh, to Switzerland, to anywhere out of the dirt and decay and chaos that she still saw in the parts of the house she hadn't tackled yet—and forgot as promptly as she could the grand house she was now mistress of.

Little by little, then, as Delia grew up, the house slid into decay even more profound. Visitors loved the hall, even the decay and the dirt. Esmé had done wonders, they said. Such charm! Esmé did not contradict. Anthony became sixty, seventy, now eighty. What was she to do when he was dead? She would be only forty-four if he died this minute. She discovered by chance that in the mid—nineteenth century the family went bankrupt after a speculative spending spree by an ambitious Quondam who wanted to make Hartland a spa after the discovery of some medicinal springs to the north of the village. He enlarged an inn, got the railway to put in a loop with a tiny station, built several decent houses that visitors could rent for a mythical season, and made a handsome bath-house in the vicinity of the springs. But the rise of nearby Harrogate aborted these schemes, and in a year or two the Quondams found they couldn't even afford the hall; so they moved to Akeld until the eldest son found an heiress to marry. Then the hall was refurbished, and most of the family shunted back to it.

Esmé wouldn't have bothered. Akeld was a very pretty house on the slope of a bank looking over the green and peaceful Swathbeck Vale. No one would quarrel with her wish to live there, but Esmé felt she had to justify it, or at least pretend that the place was wished on her. This would have the effect of freeing her from the past. If she lived another forty years, what good would it be if she was hackled with the impedimenta of the first forty?

So, long before the Amorys had done more than suggest to their closest friends that Akeld wasn't entirely meeting their needs, Esmé had called and made a sketch of what needed doing. "Anthony is thinking of transferring the estate to the girls," she explained to Lucy Amory, who was married to a racehorse trainer and bred ponies. "You probably could do with more stabling, couldn't you? Did someone tell me that you've been looking at a place near Malton?"

Lucy Amory thought she might have mentioned that she had, though to whom she was unsure. It was impossible to keep secrets in the country, and she never blamed Esmé for listening to other people's business. Esmé even seemed to be making a move easy for her by suggesting they could break the lease and agreeing on the amount of work needed at Akeld.

By the time Esmé had gone round again with the farm manager and made it clear what the estate joiner and mason and their men were to do, everyone in Hartland knew of the impending move. What a sport she was! What would old Anthony have done without her! It would be good to have children in the hall again, not just sweet Delia, but a pack of children, with their up-to-date fathers and mothers, leaders of society. And the estate might profit. Anthony was old. For many years management had been lax. Then those who worked for the estate grew anxious at the idea of working for three bosses, women at that. They thought that Anthony should have called the estate workers together and broken the news to them himself, as the grandfather did (so it had been recorded by their forefathers) when he transferred the estate to Anthony's father, two years before the old man died and a year before the young man went off to his death in France. Transfer to the heir in the owner's lifetime had been an acceptable practice for nearly a century, but it had to be done right. People understood that inheritance tax and death duties had to be avoided in the interest of the estate, and the heir had to get his hand in before the owner died, but it was common courtesy to explain the logic, and the logistics, and the policies regarding tied cottages, and insurance for the estate workers, and to hear the fears of the workers concerning the owner's liabilities. So after the preliminary excitement the village of Hartland was touched with resentment at the way a decision had been made over its head. What power the Quondams still had! It didn't seem right in this day and age. What did the village people know of Gwen and Reggie and their husbands? Delia they knew, Delia they loved, but she was young and bound to be over-ruled by the other two. Moreover, though Delia knew them, Gwen and Reggie did not. These justifiable fears were voiced again and again in local society.

4

Where did memory go when you lost it? Into nothingness? Into chaos? Into limbo, to be retrieved with tricks, or to come back spontaneously when you were thinking of something else?

Anthony Quondam was never in any doubt that the decision to leave the hall was his alone. The memory of how he had reached that decision was sharp, the occasion unforgettable. One morning about six, still night outside, he was going downstairs with the aid of a torch (so as not to waken his wife) to make tea in the kitchen, when he saw from the tall Venetian window on the stairs a light shining to the southeast, on the rim of the hill, in the distance, where he had never seen a light shine before. It gradually detached itself from the horizon, a thin curve, a pale fingernail, the newest of new moons. It travelled up through the bones of a beech tree while he stood on the stairs, minute after minute, holding the bannister. A glow appeared on its left, lighting the sky above it. Then the sun showed its red crown. Soon sun and moon shone in the twilight side by side, and the sky went mad with colours and lights. Something in the mind of the old witness twitched and slackened and lurched like a beached boat floated by the incoming tide. It was a marvellous sensation. Being at sea gave him the same burst of happiness, the sea's huge uncontrollable element rolling and tossing at its ease. How amazing that he'd never before seen moon and sun dawn side by side. The ease of nature—how wicked to forget it and allow yourself to be restricted by artificial human handcuffs and shackles! He would begin a totally different sort of life. Quite naturally and promptly he would give away the hall and the estate to the girls and become finally unencumbered. He was thrilled to think how free he would become. His spirit would soar like a flight of birds— and so of course would Esmé's.

There was another factor leading him to action. Anthony had always thought that Quondam Hall, being large and beautiful, made its inhabitants large and beautiful too, like spirits in noble bodies. He had said as much to Alice once and she had shrieked with laughter. Later she recovered and apologised. "You are right up to a point, my love; but I find the landed gentry petty and ugly rather than 'large and beautiful.'" Here again she collapsed. Alice was a robust woman; sometimes too robust. Sometimes she behaved in such a way as to drive his most idiosyncratic self underground. If he answered her smartly and clearly, she respected him, but she disliked woolliness, and half one's thoughts are woolly until hardened by talk or writing. So she was excellent for him when he was in the House. But one is not always a politician, or on show, in public, and he often felt the need to work out ideas with her; she was after all a clever and educated woman. But she could slap him down without compunction and laugh at him without a scrap of sympathy, as in the case of his theory regarding the hall's influence on the soul. Well, perhaps it was a lunatic thought. But there again, the thought of God can be lunatic. All the best ideas have a touch of the lunatic when first proposed.

Anthony never spoke of this particular idea again in case others laughed in that accusing way. Yet he was sure he was right. He had seen visitors to the hall take in the proportions of the best rooms and spontaneously move their hands over their hair to tidy it. Even the postmaster, an objective witness and one who liked to deliver his thoughts, said that people driving through the village for the first time sat up straight and blew their noses at the sight of the portals of the hall, the too tidy church, and the rows of neat stone cottages with their matching doors and flower baskets. Anthony knew why. This order, decorum, controlled idealism (whatever you liked to call it), struck at the heart. Let people snigger if they wanted. Having driven through, many people did a U-turn and drove through again. Presumably they enjoyed sitting up straight and blowing their noses, it made them proud of themselves even while they felt the weight of their exclusion.

So let his daughters take up this natural force, this ennobling ownership. That very day he telephoned his solicitors. And it was amazing to him, and yet perfectly natural too, like the rise of sun and moon side by side, or the sea, or a storm, that his decision came as no particular surprise to anybody.

All the more of a shock, then, to see his beloved Delia go mad and rush off to live in a caravan, as he'd specified in his perfectly justifiable rage—not even a proper gipsy caravan but a wheeled box set among other wheeled boxes, in a bare field. "Summer homes" was the cant description of such vile mistakes. As if the people in them hibernated elsewhere and only came "home" in the warm weather. Such mimic luxury bothered him. It was commendable to live with very little. A man of his great-grandfather's generation had set off naked into the Canadian woods at the start of winter and after six months reappeared hale and hearty—clad in skins and so forth—and won an enormous bet. If Delia left Quondam Hall and lived in a caravan, it would be more than she needed. Many were homeless and lived in shop doorways and cardboard boxes, thousands of people, thousands, thanks to the bloody present Government and their bloody ideal (*ideal!*) that successful citizens should be encouraged to get rich and be lauded thereby and the rest go to the wall, unsuccessful citizens for whom the Government had no time. A dreadful political theory, that, falsely extrapolated from Darwinian theory of evolution through the survival of the fittest. It was not Christian, it was not spiritual, it was not even human. Should he, then, Anthony Quondam, compel the needy to come in from the highways and hedgerows as people were gathered for the feast of the Kingdom of Heaven? Should he open the hall to them? He knew that they would not come. Should he permit Delia to live houseless even if she wished it? He would make her warm, he would make her beautiful, but she did not need that. She had need of nothing, and nothing was what she needed. But that was not the point, Delia.

To go back: As soon as Esmé had come down in her blue silk dressing gown, looking a bit lost, as always in the mornings, he had immediately informed her of his decision to give the hall to the girls, and she had come alive, and smoothed his hair and beard with her pretty little elegant hands, coming close so that he could smell her perfumed, still agreeable breath. Then he produced a counter-argument to entice her to still more kind gestures, as a penguin presents another penguin with a large round stone when what it desires is an egg. "They'll quarrel, of course," he said.

"No they won't," she said cheerfully.

"I wonder if they can afford it. It's time to have the roof on the west wing entirely relaid. And the chimneys over the gallery are leaning over. We must call in Dickson."

"They'll have more money than we have. They have professional incomes, and they can sell their houses and live here without mortgages or rents."

"You and I will take a few nice things and a little money to live on at Akeld."

All had seemed simple then. He envisioned a life of charm, comfort, and honour in his decent old farmhouse, all low ceilings and warmth and old oak furniture. There parcels of longed-for books would arrive and be unwrapped and opened and sampled, for Anthony loved his old library, and his private life consisted mostly of reading alone there. He would gather his notes and actually start writing his local history, in a nice leather notebook. He and Esmé would walk in the woods, benign presences in nature like obelisks and springs. The past had acted like a brake. Now he'd release it and go damn fast, being what he wanted to be, doing what he wanted to do. He saw himself (his true self) as so honest and good that honesty and goodness had to come of his actions. This would be his last chance. He had looked after the estate like an old nanny except for that awful time when he'd gambled a bit and had to let Clum go to Peter Wilson. On the whole, that hadn't mattered. Peter was a good fellow and looked after the land adequately and preserved the village and looked after his people as well as Anthony ever did. The Quondams had always managed to maintain a certain bias in favour of ordinary humanity.

Their start at Hartland had been, well, not exactly raffish, not so suspect as some, but a little shady—they were a Northumberland family who'd come south after the disaster of the Pilgrimage of Grace, when they were given a forfeited estate, the owner having to save his skin in France. By the outbreak of the Civil War a century later they'd perversely become Roman Catholic themselves, dutifully paying the fines for recusants and keeping their heads down. By the time of the Commonwealth they'd become Puritans. At the Restoration, they bobbed back to the middle and became backers of the Church of England. Later they'd weathered fifty years of Marmaduke Quondam, a lunatic, and the jolly profligacy of the next heir. It had been touch and go.

After the show-down with her father, Delia went for a long walk on the moors. As she strode out, she sang and laughed, as the moors were sunny and bright and heavy with the warmth held in the peat. When she came back to Hartland, she slipped into her barn in the early dusk and stayed there, locking the door and making do with a cup of tea for her supper. Someone came knocking quietly at the door about eight o'clock—her mother, probably, calling in her debts. Esmé was frightened of destitution in her old age, so she often called them in. Like a debtor, Delia ignored the knock and the faint voice calling over the noise of rain that had started to fall.

There was a cot in a corner of the barn so Delia could lie down and think in the middle of a painting session and even spend the night there if she wanted. There was also a lavatory and a wash-basin and a shower stall in an area curtained off by tattered stuff discarded from some bedroom. Delia had found it in the attic, and the estate carpenter had installed it for her on a semi-circular wooden rail supported by two wooden posts, for privacy. Outside this makeshift bathroom there was a similar kind of kitchen, consisting of a small refrigerator and a two-plate electric hob set on a kitchen table. In the centre of the long wall facing the door she had also put in a big spotted mirror removed from the corridor outside the servants' hall in which servants once tidied themselves before going upstairs. The mirror increased the light in the barn and would provide the painter with new perspectives of models when, as she intended, she asked people to sit for her. Hence Delia spent the night at her ease. Her one regret was that she had to leave this island of convenience and go to a place where it would be much harder to work. That, though, was attractive, too.

The next day, early, after packing half a dozen cardboard boxes with clothes and painting materials, she drove over to the caravan park hidden in the trees by Piercy Castle. It had been there some thirty years. The Piercys had put it in during the bad times when country house visiting was not the industry it had become. The site still made a worthwhile profit, according to the Piercys, like the plant nursery and the trout farm and the riding school and the forestry service and the pheasant and partridge shooting and the clay pigeon shooting and the summer concerts, all of which—with the stiff entrance fee—contributed to the maintenance of the castle and the severely reduced but still pretty grand style of its hereditary owners. But it was not a lovely thing, though neatly laid out and ostensibly practical, and there was something wrong about its temporary character, a smugness in the fiction that it was about to move on and pitch itself somewhere else, when everyone who saw it was clear that it was there to stay until it fell apart. Into the rows of empty mooring sites and past the two caravans tethered to cars, up to the half-dozen trailers permanently there and apparently closed for the winter, Delia drove looking for someone in charge. Or did caravan sites run themselves? She wasn't keen on going up to the estate office to make enquiries because she knew the man in charge, an officious ex-army type who called himself the Steward, nor would she approach the Comptroller, also known, equally officious, but a woman too, who'd instantly smell the rat of a family quarrel. Neither would understand why she wanted to rent a caravan a few miles from home. Both would reach for the telephone and consult Lady Piercy, an embarrassment so horrid Delia's palms stuck to the wheel when she thought of it. If she'd wanted to put pressure on her father, that might be a good approach, but she didn't want to press him. She had in mind a piety so profound as to set both her father and herself free from words. She thought of true obedience as absolute silence. Even now when she thought of this obedience, a sensation of peace stole into her body as if she saw a large comfortable chair being prepared for her to sit on.

"You want to know if there's a static to let?"

She had banged at the door of a trailer where a light shone in a window, and a man of about thirty appeared. He had long moustaches like an ancient Briton, and hair caught back in an elastic band. His tone was indignant. People didn't let statics. Anyway, who'd let a static to a young woman straight off the street? "That's a pretty amazing thing to ask," he said, laughing to show how loony her request was. "What's your name, where you from?" The answers didn't matter. He was thinking of a way to let her down gently. She looked nice. In fact, she was very pretty. Pretty girls didn't often come to the caravan site. Certainly none of them wanted to rent a caravan. On the whole, people who used the site were a hundred years old or young married couples with kids. He wondered if she was on the run from the police. He came down the steps of the trailer and stood on the bald trampled ground next to her with his hands stuck into the back pockets of his jeans. Their eyes were on a level. Delia was tall for a woman. Like him, she wore jeans and an old shirt under a sweat shirt. She too stuck her hands in her back pockets and they swayed towards each other and away like pigeons in a town square.

When she told him her name he said, "I'm Tom Charlton," nodded, then added, "I'm from Newcastle." As far as he was concerned, that was news. He had been born and brought up in the city and only discovered nature on a day trip to the castle ten summers ago. The discovery changed his life. The Piercys had put him in charge of the caravans after finding him sleeping rough in the Temple of Temperance. In spite of his hair, he'd done well. If Lady Piercy kept referring to him as a rough diamond, it was only to save her prejudices, in much the same way as the local people made fun of his Geordie accent. They were amused by the passion of his bird-watching and badger protecting and knowledge of foxes, and how he fussed over the maintenance of rights of way across the countryside. When he heard talk of the transfer of the Quondam estate from father to daughters, the same interest was aroused. The idea that the owner of a fine old house should surrender it to a younger generation, and lassies at that, struck him, predictably, as plain noble. And now this windfall of a girl.

When she said she was Delia Quondam and lived at Hartland, he was shocked all the same at how young she was. She was the old man's youngest, of course, but she could have been his great-granddaughter. Men of sixty had children, yes. Always supposing she was his. The oldest man admitted by English courts to have sired an heir was a Lord Whatnot aged eighty-four, though that was before DNA and even blood sampling. (He had looked this up in the York County Library.)

"What do you want it for, then?" he asked, knowing she had that vast place at home to play hide-and-seek in.

She said she wanted somewhere on her own for a few weeks.

"I know what you mean," he said.

This was dubious. His own loneliness must be of a different order. He was on his own far too much; that was the snag with being manager of a caravan site at the back end of the year. The Piercys might as well close the place down for the winter, except for the birdwatchers or walkers who'd drive out from little places in Leeds or Bradford or even Huddersfield or Middlesbrough.

"I'm a painter," she said, "I'm painting landscapes of the park. I want to observe the landscape right through the day without coming and going."

"You could just as soon get over here every day by bike." He was only trying to help. He repeated, "I know what you mean." He was a great believer in hard looking. For that you needed to be on the spot. It wouldn't be the same, biking. The idea of having a painter at work next door was grand. He was learning to put words together, himself.

Then suddenly he knew he was going to give her what she wanted. Why not? Her family wasn't going to disappear, and he was all for youngsters making their own way and learning to be independent, especially if they were lassies. He decided which was the best of the statics and rang up the owner, who agreed to lease by the week to such a reliable customer. It was better for the caravan to be lived in than left uninhabited. An unattractive time of year, the back end, Michaelmas, muck-spreading time, muddy, smelly, cold; the owner wasn't planning a visit soon.

There was no hint that the caravan owner wanted his money immediately, which was as well, because Delia had very little. Her college grant had come to an end the previous summer with the acquisition of her degree, and she had been living on hand-outs from her father. She had been deciding how to earn her living while continuing to paint, and the decision had been put off and put off as she worked on her paintings in the comfort of the great barn. The rent of the static was very little, and nothing compared with what she paid in her last year of college for a small room in Islington. "I'd like to give you a week's rent now," she told Tom. "And I'd like to move in today." She hoped he would not bring up the question of a deposit, and for the moment he did not.

They were standing in the static and Delia gradually became radiant with relief and hope. Tom had gone over the place thoroughly, explaining how each bit worked. She was lucky, he said; the wife here was an excellent housekeeper and you could eat off the floor. They both looked at the floral carpet, grinning. He opened a cupboard and revealed spotless sheets, two snowy pillows, a duvet in a plastic bag. "Ideal," Delia said. "I never knew." She unfolded and folded the bunks, the table. She peered through the windows. She said, "My ideal house up to now has been ecologically sound—that was the basis; a space cut into a berm . . ."

"Oh ay? Berm?"

"A bank—bank walls on three sides, with twenty inches of heavy insulation against the bare earth and in the roof, which would run out from the top of the berm to cover the cavity. South facing, plenty of glass to let in the sun, but with overhanging eaves to prevent over-heating in the summer. Log-burning stove. Back-up central heating. Cheap to run. From a distance you wouldn't even see it. A static is just the opposite, really. I'm not sure that I don't prefer it."

"Oh, ay?" Tom was smitten with admiration. This thinking went far beyond his. "How did you start on a train of thought that would lead up to a berm, a house in a berm?"

"Better than tree houses, and a lot less visible." Delia nearly added that her many tree houses and bolt-holes in attics and stables and woods had all been constructed with the one aim of getting away from her mother.

Tom kicked the metal door of the static and produced a ping. "I know what you mean."

"I think you do." She paid the first week's rent. She asked about electricity bills and the nearest post office. She put on a show of being businesslike to conceal a growing agony about where to find more money. She might sell her nice girl's pearls, an unwelcome present on her sixteenth birthday. She might borrow. Not from her father and mother. Certainly not from Gwen or Reggie, who probably at that very minute were crowding into her barn with their husbands and children to look at her paintings and open her sketchbooks and finger her paints and tools and read her journals and letters. The Bowerses and the Smiths were to lose no time in moving in, according to Gwen. They'd move in "lock, stock, and barrel," in Gwen's pseudo-dynamic phrasery. Disinherited? Hard cheese.

Tom made out a receipt and handed over keys and she drove off to the nearest village to buy instant coffee and milk and bread and eggs and jam and tomatoes and bacon. After she'd eaten, the long-term worries receded. It had been most satisfactory to cook a simple meal in the kitchenette of the static. But how about bringing the boxes of clothes and work materials over from Hartland? Her car was so small that she would have to make two trips, and entering the hall for her stuff would mean running into her parents and her sisters not once but twice, and getting involved in a reconciliation. Then Tom Charlton came knocking to see if she was settling down and all was well. Soon she was using the telephone in his trailer—the only private one on the site—and Tom was outside in the rain pretending not to overhear, though he was already inexplicably hurt at the idea that in her new life there were other human beings besides himself. Delia saw and understood. "I was calling my friend William Piercy at the castle," she said as she left the trailer. "He's going to get my things for me. He's got a Land Rover. I couldn't get them in my car, it's not big enough."

Tom, who spent so much time alone doing battle on nature's behalf, barely understood how Delia could perceive his pain and promptly relieve it. "Right, then," he said, cheered up.

Delia had laid sheets of heavy plastic on the spare bunk and the card-board boxes went on top. "Nice, isn't it," she said to William Piercy.

William, who was thirty and a tough-minded television producer, thought the place a blot and said so. He was also far from pleased at

Anthony Quondam's treatment of Delia, whom he wanted to marry. His annoyance took the form of displeasure with Delia.

"Anthony thinks you're out to shame him" he said.

"How's that? I did as he told me to do."

"He sees he was wrong. He was relying on you to see that. Remiss of you. How could you have let him down. I'm not kidding."

"How about Mum?"

"She says Anthony lost control. She thinks it's very clever of you to have found a caravan so quickly. She says she wouldn't have known where to begin."

"I dare say."

"Esmé's having the time of her life."

"How Dad could ever have thought a caravan was a punishment, I can't imagine. I think it's bliss. So very practical."

"I can't think why you didn't come right over and see me. You knew I was here till Thursday."

"Well, he did specify a caravan when he told me to get out, and then I knew you were working on your script, and most important of all, there's your mother. It would have been extremely awkward for her, an old friend of Dad's . . ."

"She knows him."

"But Dad would be terribly embarrassed, don't you see, if he knew I'd taken refuge with your mother."

"And you don't want to embarrass him, after he's thrown you out? You have to learn to play the game. Mother will be most hurt at your not coming to us. I know you want to be on your own, but this is one time you need friends, and especially me. You need me, Delia, though not nearly as much as I need you. Where are you going to put all this stuff, and where will you find room for your painting? I wish you'd come and live with me in Leeds, it would be much simpler and a lot more fun."

"But William, I don't want to live in Leeds, I want to live in Glasgow or London, where the interesting painting is at the moment, and I have to be on my own."

They had run through this argument before, and the discussion never advanced. At some future moment, they both understood, the sticking point would be removed by force and they would be together, possibly in one of the purlieus of Piercy Castle, where William, a younger son, still kept his rooms. Meanwhile, William saw good reason to keep the pressure up. "Do you know that when I went for your things Reggie asked me what right I had to remove them?"

"She is vile."

"I was ferrying your stuff to the Land Rover when she turned up and said, 'I hope you know what you are doing.' I said I wondered if anybody knew what they were doing. The place is in chaos. Your father and mother seem to have been taken by surprise. Everything is happening very quickly after those years of talk, and they're not ready. There were packing cases everywhere—in the hall, the stairway, the salon. I gather Anthony and Esmé are staying till Akeld is ready. But there's been trouble about what Esmé's been allowed to take—she and Anthony, I mean."

"*Allowed?*"

"Reggie and Gwen appear to think that the furniture in the hall, all of it, goes with the hall. Esmé had her eye on one or two pieces in her bedroom. And her bed. And some things she brought down from Scotland when she married. A nice little desk . . . a dozen plain little chairs with comfortable seats that she had packed away in the old kitchen, and a round mahogany table. And a sofa, and a settee. The big oak table in the old servants' hall. 'No you don't,' says Reggie, 'they belong here.' 'But they're mine,' says Esmé. 'I bought all those things. We're not taking the tapestries, or the Constable, or the Van Dyck. Just my own things and a few others that we've never used all the time we've been here.' Some were in the attic, I gather. 'And anyway,' she says, 'they'll all be yours again when we're dead.' Then Reggie goes into fits of laughter. 'What are you saying,' she says, 'you're my age, you'll outlive us all.' That's Esmé's story. She was very upset."

"He won't stand for it."

"That's not all. Gwen came roaring into the drawing-room where Esmé and I were talking. She was blind with rage. She wanted to know how many shirts I had. 'Shirts?' I said. 'Yes, shirts, how many do you own?' 'Oh, six or seven,' I said. She said, 'Do you know how many shirts my father has? Eighty. All hand-made for him by Hilditch and Key. The best shirts in the world.'"

61

"And he needs them all. I hope you told her so. He has very long arms, and a big chest, and narrow waist—a fine figure for an old man. He needs properly tailored shirts."

"And thirty suits he never wears. According to Gwen. She was shouting when she told me, as if it was my fault, or perhaps Esmé's."

"That's not many," said Delia. "Thirty suits is not very many for a man who has lived for a long time in the public eye. Did you tell her?"

"Not a chance. She told me the tailors—a dozen by Huntsman, two by So-and-So—I hadn't heard of them, but they were all famous names, so Gwen said. It mattered to her a great deal."

"And to him. He likes to be well turned out."

"Then she started on his shoes. Shirts, suits, then shoes. While she and Reggie were living in York with Alice wondering how to make ends meet, Anthony was ordering hand-made shoes from Lobb. 'Do you know how many pairs of shoes I had when I was a schoolgirl? Two. And that old fart had forty. FORTY. All beautiful, beautiful hand-made shoes.'"

"She didn't call him that?"

"Sweet Delia, you need never see her again. I said to your mother, 'Esmé, we don't have to listen to this.' 'Yes you do,' yelled Gwen. 'You'll damn well listen, God damn you.' And Anthony came in."

"The noise, I suppose," said Delia. "He doesn't like women to shout. He doesn't shout, himself, not ever have I known him to do so." As soon as she spoke, she remembered how he had shouted at her in her barn the previous day. But in principle, she told herself, in principle he did not shout. And she was aware of her prejudice in his favour.

"He said to Gwen, 'Who in God's name are you? Certainly no daughter of mine!' And she roared back at him, and he cursed her. I didn't know men could curse their daughters. He cursed her womb. She laughed and said, bad luck, she wasn't having more children anyway. He said he hoped Julian and Clare would stamp on her face. Esmé shrieked and shrieked. Gwen shouted, 'Where are we going to put his wardrobe till he goes to Akeld? Akeld won't be big enough to hold it. And his books. And his tools. And Esmé! And *her* things!'"

"Poor mother. She brought it on herself."

"Esmé was always kind to me when I was a boy, at dinner parties, when I had nothing to say until she talked to me."

"Oh, she can be kind, yes."

"A lot of jealousy there, on your sisters' part. I don't think your mother had any idea. Nor your father, of course. Was *he* unkind?"

"No, never." Again she was aware that she was not quite owning up to the truth.

"I forgot to say that in the middle of the explosion, Gwen's husband walked in. What a fool. He was keen on getting everyone to calm down. 'Shut up,' says Gwen without listening. 'Get back to your work-bench. Make me a chair, I need one, they're stripping the place, and it's so run-down,' she says, 'we'll have to work like dogs to put it to rights.'"

"It's not like Gwen to rant and roar. She keeps professional." She remembered something. "But she told me once that anger should be expressed openly. It sounded OK. So was she doing herself some good? Do you know what Gwen said to me once? I was about ten. She'd been telling me how pretty I was, and explaining that was why Father loved me. She said she was not pretty, and therefore Father did not love her. It didn't sound quite true, and I knew she was talking down. It was too difficult to argue. She said, 'I may be plain, but the moment I open my mouth, people listen.'"

"Do they?"

"I don't know. The point was that she was expressing what she saw as the truth and putting me straight. Oh, I dare say it's true. I dare say they listen. She's even become loved. She has her husband and children, and people she counsels. They must love her."

"She said to Anthony just now, 'When did you last speak to anyone? You never speak to me.' It was sad. He didn't say anything. And then she said, 'I have to make my own life. You can curse me if you want.' 'I do curse you,' he shouted. And Gwen said in a thoughtful voice, 'If I had your power, I'd behave quite differently.'"

"I dare say she would."

"She has ideas about running the hall that have nothing to do with Anthony."

"What ideas?"

"She said that long ago when she and Reggie were young things and you were a baby, you'd gone to sleep on his lap, passed out, she said, like one of those doped Gipsy beggar children on the doorstep of an Italian church, with purple eyelids and dead pale skin, who jerk the heartstrings of foreign visitors and loosen their purse strings. Anthony was so pleased at the time that he could hardly breathe. And Gwen said now that she thought Esmé had arranged 'the tableau.' He never cradled Reggie and her like that. Esmé said, 'You wouldn't remember it if he did. You see conspiracy everywhere.'"

"Gwen thinks men are a conspiracy," said Delia.

"Are we?" He took her hand.

"Father's pretty comic, the way he expects me to fall over myself with adoration for him. He wants me to be a puppy dog so he can carry me everywhere. Sometimes he even calls me Esmé."

"That's disgusting!"

"It is, rather, isn't it. I wish he'd go away and leave me alone. Nothing is enough for him."

"He didn't have to throw you out, though."

"It was a natural response. I took him seriously. Gwen and Reggie didn't even begin to take him seriously. They laugh at him. They'd say anything he wanted. They don't care what he wants, the answer would always be yes. I think he's a threat. When I was little, he'd take me by the hand through the woods and name all the flowers and show me the old stone boundary markers, and when I was tired, he would put me on his shoulders and climb Knob Bank where we'd look over the valley, and he'd name the hills and farms for me as if he was God handing out creation to Adam."

William opened two cans of beer from the six-pack he'd brought. "Gwen said something pretty remarkable. She's a pretty remarkable lady all round, your eldest sister. She said that Esmé never wanted you and that she tried to abort you, but Anthony saved you. That's why you are the favourite."

Delia paused. "A lot of women *think* about getting rid of their babies. What's wrong with that?"

"I gather it was very important indeed at the time. Esmé wanted to go into a clinic and have a proper abortion, not just jump down the stairs or drink a bottle of gin. And Anthony went mad with grief, so she changed her mind. She was very young, wasn't she? Delia . . ."

As he hugged her and she wept, he said that Gwen had added in pure spite that Esmé probably wanted an abortion because the baby wasn't Anthony's. That's when he himself had turned on his heel and marched out.

"I'm not Anthony's? How absurd."

"Don't take any notice of her."

"I don't look very like him. Perhaps I'm not. Whose am I, then, if not his? How interesting!"

"She's a spiteful bitch, and you left just in time. The world is coming apart. She wants to disinherit you, love."

"But Anthony has disinherited me already."

"I doubt if that can be done so soon. But she certainly wants your share. She and Reggie are going to turn the hall into a business with fifty thousand customers a year. I'm not kidding. It'll cost millions. And where the money's going to come from, I can't imagine, nor can they. 'Everyone does it,' Gwen said. 'You do it,' she said to me. I couldn't say that we do it a bit less blatantly than that, though perhaps we try to."

He hugged her again. "Look, let's get married right away. You can't go on living here."

"But I love it here!" She was surprised. They sat on the floral carpet and kissed. Then they heard a car draw up outside, and someone ran up the steps and knocked sharply and Esmé's voice cried out, "Are you there, Delia? It's Mum. Delia?"

"Hush," Delia whispered. They lay entwined on the floor until they heard the footsteps resound on the metal steps, the car door slam, the motor burst alive and rev, and the car dash off. She started to giggle. Serve Esmé right. She'd come to the caravan expecting Delia to go back with her. She'd have said, "Goodness, you mustn't take your father so seriously! Yes, yes, he told you to go and live in a caravan, and you did that, quite right. Now come back, he's feeling very very sorry."

"God what a fool she is, poor thing," Delia said.

"She saw our cars outside and was embarrassed. She knew we were here. Poor Esmé."

"I know."

5

The hills near Hartland and Piercy Castle were walking country, famous for the woods and wild flowers and views and ancient farms that appeared unexpectedly among their banks and vales. Only the tracks saved the walker in such convoluted scenery from total confusion. Many tracks were very old and therefore sunken, running just below the top of ridges or diving across them, once in a while accompanying prehistoric earthen ramparts of mysterious utility. One track led Delia down a bank in a series of wriggles to a concealed bog, which it crossed by means of an ancient grassy causeway to a small bridge over a beck. Though in the middle of nowhere, the bridge was elaborately and finely made, a narrow arch of stone and brick as high as ten feet above the busy water. Delia examined it from the side and underneath and covered several pages of her sketchbook with illustration.

Further along the beck, there were other delights. The track fell to the right along a wood, isolating an old oak at the corner. Once there had been a great forest of oaks here. This one survived as a huge trunk without a canopy. Only a few limbs remained, sticking out like sets of forearms but with enough leaf litter underneath to show the trunk was thriving. Delia's fingertips prickled. She sat down and began to sketch.

She had been out sketching every day for weeks. It was terrible being a novice, but not quite as terrible as it had been. She had always drawn and painted well, but there was a chasm between what she could do and what she wanted to do, and the signs of it closing were a delight. She got up early every day and put a thermos of tea and some bread and cheese in a sack with her sketching materials and dressed herself in thermal underwear, trousers, quilted jacket, boots with two pairs of socks, and set out, not to return to the static till after dark. Her passion possessed her as she exercised it. There was nothing to stop her. William went back to Leeds with his script for weeks at a time, returning at intervals to hole up with her. There was no reason why she couldn't live like this for months, apart from poverty. She refused to take money from her lover, and unfortunately he couldn't find her pearls, as they were kept in her bedroom upstairs in the hall, and he hadn't the face to butt through the house demanding directions. On every visit he reported further terrible clashes between her sisters and her parents, which fixed Delia's resolve not to go near the hall. She could imagine being attacked by Gwen and Reggie for showing her face. Then her parents might fall on her neck, which would irritate her, and her nieces and nephew would giggle and cry at the very sight of her. Ridiculous Billy Bowers might be nice, but he didn't count. Jeremy Smith, her other brother-in-law, counted, but was seldom at home. It was a pity about money, as she was coming to the point of wishing to use oils, which were expensive. Meantime whole paintable compositions lay, as it were, in the palm of her open clutching hand. She filled five sketchbooks and began a sixth.

When all her cash was gone, she drove to York and stripped her small bank account. She bought food and some washing powder and several small canvases and some oils and had twenty pounds left. The second instalment of rent for the static was due, and so of course was the deposit. It would be nice to obey her father as elegantly and precisely as Esmé evaded all obligations. That meant not taking money from her mother. She was not worried about her parents. She thought they would manage the move to Akeld eventually. The future didn't interest her any more than that. Its void merely made clear what was alive and important now. If they knew what was good for them, Anthony and Esmé would move to Akeld and camp in the decorators' debris, simply commandeering beds and linen and what furniture they needed from the hall. The countryside would not stand for an open battle between Anthony Quondam and his two elder daughters, least of all a battle in which other people had to take sides. Anthony had authority, the daughters didn't. Told by Anthony what to take, the mover's men would take those things, however often the order was countermanded by the women. Delia saw nothing to worry about.

On the other hand, she was unsure of detail. What about Jack and Helen Thwaite, who acted as butler and housekeeper and occupied a pleasant flat over the stables? They had been with Anthony and Esmé since she was ten. Would they stay on? What about William Sykes, the gardener, who occupied a lodge? What about the tenant farmers and the foresters and the gamekeepers, who owed some loyalty to the old man? Recent events had reduced him pitifully. Would they be sorry or glad? You never knew the resentments in a village. Divorce and gambling debts and the loss of Clum were mentioned like the names of old battles, but the reign of Esmé had brought a lifetime of peace. "Your father's very popular," people told her. But was it true? William had said something about carrying the old man out of burning Troy. After thinking about it for weeks, Delia decided she had better walk over the fields to Akeld and find out what was going on there from the workmen Esmé had sent in.

She took her time strolling along the ridge and down the back way to Akeld. To her surprise it was deserted. The old stone sink in the kitchen had been ripped out and lay in the lilacs on the edge of the garden. Peering through the windows, Delia saw that a new stainless steel one had been installed, together with expensive-looking cupboards and shelves, a matching cooker and refrigerator, a blue Aga, and a new tiled floor. The doors were locked, but she found the upper part of the pantry window open and managed to squeeze through after levering herself up via an old wheelbarrow left standing in the garden. The painting and wallpapering and carpeting in the rest of the house had not started, which was astonishing considering for how long and with what detail Esmé had laid her plans. Perhaps they were waiting for the electrician to put in the new wiring, or the man to put in the double glazing, or the plumber to tie in the new kitchen appliances and perhaps a new bathroom. Or were her parents out of ready money? It was a mystery.

There was a wonderful view over the vale from the southern windows. Woods crowded behind the house and on either side, making a harbour in which the house rode in a little clear bay of grass. To the south was a broad terrace, and below it again more woodland. Now that the foliage was gone you could see paths and seats and rocks in the woods that made it deeply satisfying to walk there. Delia's eyes sought a fine, tall oak that she used to play in when visiting an aunt of her father's who used to live at Akeld when Delia was small. It was not visible. Could the October winds have blown it down? In fact, all the oaks that gave Akeld its name seemed to have dipped out of sight. She was scrambling out of the pantry window again, determined to investigate, when she heard the noise of a car's wheels on the gravel, and just had time to drop down in the deep grass beside the wheelbarrow and hide before Esmé drove up. Tom Charlton of the caravan park was seated beside her. The car passed to the front of the house and after a pause a key rattled in the front door.

"You see what a mess we're in here," came Esmé's voice, flurried but precise, helpless but determined, magnified by the uncurtained empty rooms. "Now you just see what you can do about the water and the electricity, Mr. Charlton. It really is too bad. I'm very cross with Mrs. Smith, my stepdaughter. She cannot have a notion of the inconvenience she is causing. I'm impatient to move in, but I've never used any but the estate workmen, and I don't know where to look for other workmen as reliable as they are. That's stupid of me, isn't it. What do other people do, you'll say. It's a matter of what one is used to. Well, if we can just move in and camp, that'll be better than what we have at present. Mr. Quondam is very upset."

Heavy footfalls began to march to and fro, and at the level of Delia's ear a series of clicks and burbles broke out, followed by a gush.

"Oh!" shrieked Esmé. "You are a genius, a perfect genius!"

Tom Charlton's voice then declared manfully that water was bursting all over the kitchen floor. He said he'd best turn it off. The washer was not tied in. The gush ceased. "A bit of a flood," Tom said. "Here's a bucket." The bucket clanged, and clanged several more times. "It's no good, it's not going to work, you can't live here until the water's tied in. I don't dare find the mains for the power. It won't be safe." In the voice of common sense, "I'd a thought there was room enough at the hall for you and Mr. Quondam, a great house like that. Or you could move to a hotel."

"You don't know my husband. That's what my other stepdaughter, Mrs. Bowers, said: 'Move to a hotel!' There was a tremendous scene when she said that to my husband. We were on the verge of a punch-up." Esmé laughed a little. "Mr. Bowers taking his wife's part, you know, my husband ready to hit him on the nose. Very unseemly at his age. Tom, Mr. Charlton, I mean, were you ever married?"

What cheek, Delia thought.

"Married and divorced," came the voice of Tom, matter-of-factly.

"Were you, now, were you. I thought you had a way of taking command, Mr. Charlton, and I was right, was I not."

If he can swallow flattery like that, he's a dead man, Delia thought.

"Well, you know how difficult life can be when you and your partner are on different wavelengths. My husband insists on his due. And it was unfortunate in a way that Mrs. Bowers sold her house so promptly and decided to move her family into the hall before we were ready. Because Mrs. Smith did not want to be outdone and she too moved her family to the hall, even though her house in Harrogate remains to be sold. This is confidential, Mr. Charlton."

Burbles of reassurance followed.

"So," said Esmé, "Mrs. Bowers, who is a professional woman, has taken three months' leave to settle her family in, and of course Mrs. Smith is anxious to be no less settled, and that's why she got the workmen from Akeld to go right over to the hall and do whatever is necessary there immediately."

"I wouldn't say that was right," said Tom in his deepest voice.

"No," said Esmé in a quiet voice. "I am very sad at what has happened."

"Your own daughter is well out of it, then. Delia, isn't it? I'll watch her, Mrs. Quondam. You've no need to worry there." Delia gnashed her teeth. It was a blessing she had left the hall, but she had not gone far enough away. She might even have to move away from William. The only trouble lay in making her money last. "It's a very nice house, is this."

"Isn't it *lovely?* I've always longed to live here."

Poor sweet Mum, thought Delia. Why on earth did you marry

Anthony? You could have married anyone you wanted. His adoration must have lain on you like a stone.

They began to discuss Esmé's plans for each room, moving out of earshot to the far end of the house and then upstairs. If Delia made a break for it, they would see her from the upper windows, so she lay low, hoping they would not make a tour round the outside when they'd finished indoors. Presently there came the slam of the front door and, after she felt a moment's apprehension that they'd come in sight, the sound of the car starting and moving off over gravel again. Delia ran straight into the woods towards Piercy Castle, not up the hill as she had come, and so for the first time saw that the oaks below Akeld, which someone had planted two centuries ago in artistic clumps, had all been felled and lay like vast segments of Stonehenge in a litter of their own branches.

As Delia stared disbelieving at the devastation, her father walked over the park at Hartland with his three dogs on leads, jostling one another and wondering why they could not run free—the old cairn, Lizzie, and the two Labradors, Nero and Jackdaw. Anthony walked fast, ignoring the gambolling that Lizzie went in for now and then when she saw a space in front of her not occupied by the large plodding Labradors. That morning he and Esmé had been in Delia's barn, sitting side by side on the extra cot that had been brought in, and drinking coffee made on Delia's two-plate hob, when Gwen had come storming in without so much as a knock or halloo, throwing open the door and shouting and crying, kicking at the old cairn that went running to greet her so that poor Lizzie sailed through the air yelping, and went on yelping as she landed, limping and falling in her haste to get out of Gwen's way. The Labradors, till then asleep on Delia's own cot, leapt up barking and growling and went at Gwen—whom they barely knew—with their black otter hair bristling.

"What, in God's name, is going on?" Anthony had said, rising with difficulty from the low cot, wiping his mouth, calling off the Labradors, calming Nero with a hand on his side, whistling to Lizzie, who was now frolicking, anxious to compensate for displeasing, unsure of the correct response. And the master was himself unsure, pausing

at the sight of the beserk woman yowling with her mouth open, showing the fillings in her back teeth and the uvula wobbling at the back
of the throat.

"Calm down! Let's be calm!" Esmé had cried, rising from the cot
like a moth in her pale silky wrap. "Be calm, Gwen. Sit down. Sit on
this cushion. Drink this coffee. We can put matters right. What has
happened, tell us." (Gwen, with those teeth bared and that mouth
and those brandishing arms, a perfect baboon. Painful for him to see,
as the baboon's father.)

"Your dogs, your senile incontinent dogs, like you, old shit, incontinent." (Almost funny. One ignores such intemperance, one pre-
tends not to hear, one tries not to smile.)

"Why, Gwen, my dear!"

"Your pack of foul-smelling bloody curs have beshat my drawing-
room." (My drawing-room? Yes, strictly it was hers, forfeited by Delia.
What had Delia done wrong? Oh, nothing, my Delia. But Delia was
banished and the baboon had moved in.) "The stench! The abomi-
nation! And they sleep in your bed, no wonder you smell, with your
appalling old man's smell, your smelly body and smelly clothes, the
hall smells from one end to another."

"Honestly, Gwen."

"Oh, *shut up,* you bloody bitch!"

"Oh, Gwen." Esmé trembled.

"Wheest, woman." (He was repeating a joke phrase of Esmé's, a
phrase she used to rebuke herself. Unsuitable for this occasion, but he
could think of no other.)

"Don't tell me what to do, you old fool! My behaviour has meaning. The dogs' behaviour has meaning: they shit all over the drawing-
room floor to show defiance and to assert themselves. The ultimate in
insult. Prisoners smear their faeces on walls. It's infantilism. Regres-
sive behaviour. I blame you." For a time it seemed that textbook
analysis would lead to textbook calm. Esmé drew in her breath and let
it sigh out. But Gwen had not so much as begun the tale of the dogs'
iniquity. Her voice, which had sunk to accommodate theory, rose to
express fury. "Clare, jumping downstairs as a child will, was set on
and bitten by those mouldy-toothed old creatures, those Labradors
there. They should have been put down long ago, like you, you blith-
ering old fool."

"Labradors don't set on children! I don't believe you!"

"It happened. The two of them got excited—dogs are pack animals at heart, you're always telling me . . . ."

"Oh Gwen! You must do something, Anthony. Dogs don't understand when they're made to move, when they're displaced, you see, poor Gwen, and poor, poor Clare. We'll go instantly and make amends to poor Clare, and is she much hurt, Gwen?"

"The brutes must be put down."

"What, my dog Nero, my dog Jackdaw? That is idiocy."

"Then it's the police. I'll tell them myself. I'll call York. They know who I am."

And then Gwen had given way even more, if such a thing were possible, and howled again, head clutched, face and neck bright red. (And this woman was supposed to be a counsellor?)

"God help us, get out of my house, what remains of my house that I have so foolishly given to you, and we shall leave, your stepmother and I, as soon as I can find somewhere else to live." (And Esmé now crying, and how prettily she did it, the Pekingese eyes like wet black marble, and the ugly daughter's eyes hidden with rolls of flesh as she bawled.) "God damn you!" Anthony bellowed.

So that was why he was taking out old Lizzie the cairn, his favourite, and the two Labradors he'd trained himself, Nero and Jackdaw, in their prime, walking them into Hartland High Wood. There he tied the Labradors to a fence post and told them to stay, and took Lizzie to an overgrown disused quarry where his forebear got the stone to build Quondam Hall. The quarry was wired off because stone occasionally fell off the quarried face, but he cut the wire with the cutters he usually carried and twisted the wire back on itself. Inside, at a cavernous opening in the rock, he fixed Lizzie's attention on a rabbit hole, and when she was peering down it, shot her in the back of the head with a pistol. He did the same with Nero and then Jackdaw. The first report had got the Labradors wagging and bristling with excitement, but the second one told Nero what was happening and he trembled so much that his hide shook, and though Anthony did not let him see the corpses of the other dogs, he must have smelled their blood, because he was howling when Anthony shot him.

Anthony dragged the bodies one after the other into the cave and piled stones on them until they were buried. He was completely composed, but he ran with sweat as he hadn't for years. He noted his sweat; one did not sweat much when old. And yet, according to Gwen, one stank. One could believe her, or not, according to whether one was going to give way to her or not. This shooting was the last time he would give way to her, and yet it was more than a giving way, it was defiance, like the killing of your own children to prevent them from falling into the hands of the enemy. He thought Gwen's Julian and Clare would criticise her for bringing about the death of the old dogs, because to any sane eye it was a pitiful thing. He was a decent boy, Julian, and his grandfather wished he had handed over the estate to him outright, with the weight of tradition behind him. His grandfather had handed over the estate to his father when he was sixty, and Anthony would have been prepared to do the same if he'd had sons. But there was difficulty over the girls, with Delia being only a child when Gwen and Reggie were in their twenties. But if he had made Julian his heir there wouldn't be trouble now, Delia would still be here and the other two putting up with their lot.

He remembered that the solicitor was still drawing up the transfer papers, taking his sweet time about it as solicitors did. He wondered if it was worthwhile trying to renounce the present situation. It would mean entering into elaborate negotiations with the lawyers. There would be unpleasant publicity, and no doubt Reggie would try and sue. And she would be right. Reggie wasn't as bad as Gwen. A more human creature altogether. A man's word was his bond, she would say, and she would be right. It was too late. Put up and shut up. He let the idea drop out of fatigue.

The old quarry was on the hillside looking over to Clum. When he was walking back to the hall, carrying the collars and leads, he met Jack Sutcliffe, his retired gamekeeper, and told him what he'd done—some explanation had to be forthcoming about his walking without dogs, with a pistol, as if he were out to do away with himself. "I'd have taken 'em, Anthony," the man remonstrated, and Anthony had touched his arm and gone on, head down, like Captain Oates in the painting, to have the other follow him and unload *his* grievances. So eventually everyone would know what had happened to the dogs, and how Gwen had complained of their smell and bad habits, and their hair on the carpets, and their number, and the price of keeping such old beasts while some children didn't have enough to eat, and of course the attack on Clare and the fouling of the drawing-room. And most insulting of all, the silly explanation in behavioural terms.

"They were protesting," Jack Sutcliffe said. "It doesn't do to leave your own place." And when Anthony said nothing, "Gwen—Mrs. Bowers—has given me notice to leave my cottage. Now I've retired, she says, she'd like me to go into a smaller place. She wants to sell my cottage. She says we can have Tufts Cottage. Very pokey and damp is Tufts."

"I dare say. Delia is in a caravan. My wife and I are moving out of the hall, I wish I knew where. No, Akeld isn't ready. Reggie's called the men into the hall to do work there first."

"I hear they've had the oaks at Akeld clear-felled. Should fetch a penny. And I'm told the little statue of the two hosses fighting, the one you're fond of, Anthony, is going to auction in London. Didn't a king give that to your ancestor?"

Anthony stopped and pretended to look at something across the vale. They stood there for ten minutes, Anthony's jaws munching, and the keeper peering into his face.

The hall had become unbearable, even Delia's barn where he was fairly private. Esmé went out every day. He sat alone in the barn, he who'd been active all his life. He read newspapers, wrote letters, called up firms about the work at Akeld. Above all, he missed his library and the books he could lay his hands on at a second's notice. Time collapsed on itself like a black hole, dense, impenetrable. One day he walked over to Clum. It was no good, though. Outrage went with him. The oddity of walking without a dog made him light-headed. He realised that he was carrying the dog leads out of habit. He didn't remember ever walking out without a dog. Lizzie might have lived to a really good age. She could have seen him out. Mary Scott of Winton had a cairn that lived to be twenty. And of course the labs were young fellows, in their prime.

"No, Akeld isn't ready," he told Peter Wilson, who was astonished at the change in his appearance. Anthony was determined to avoid a discussion of what was going on at the hall, but couldn't prevent himself from broaching the underlying issue. "Calvert's well, is he, and Gretchen? And how about Stephen? Tell me, Peter, you never thought of adopting a girl instead of a boy? Am I wrong, or are girls more difficult than boys?"

"I had no choice, Anthony." Peter eyed him diffidently. He felt an impulse to give his suffering friend something discreditable of his very own as a present. He knew, as by now everyone in the neighbourhood knew, of Reggie and Gwen's blazing rows with their father and of Delia's banishment. "A son, you see, was what we were given. I'm talking about Stephen."

"Given by the orphanage people, you mean."

"Not exactly. Well, you might as well hear the whole story now that Jess is dead. She made me swear not to tell anyone, but I never thought it mattered that much. Stephen's got on all right. The thing is, he's mine. Not Jess's. Calvert is Jess's. Stephen's by a German girl, when I was in Berlin after the war. When he came along, I adopted him."

Anthony was mildly interested. "The mother was your girl? In your office perhaps, or out in the field working for you?"

"That makes me into a pimp. That's how it appeared, I'm sure. She worked in the Russian sector as an interpreter—she'd grown up on the eastern borders of Poland, so she knew Russian, and Polish, and German, and English. She used to come over on the U-Bahn, as you could in those days, before the wall. With information, yes, in return for food and other favours. I as good as bought her. Not very nice, is it. Things were pretty bad. I used to take her to the Kempinski and she'd dress up with clothes I'd bring her, and we'd have an expensive dinner in the restaurant—my Lord, the risks she took!—and spend the night, and in the morning she'd put on her wretched old outfit again and go back to the East. She was a beautiful girl, highly intelligent."

"And Jess took the child?"

"I was in trouble by that time, trouble of a different sort. When she found she was pregnant, I got her over to the West, where she could be taken care of, and just at the time Stephen was born one of my agents was killed while he was working for me. I sent him in. My decision, and, as it turned out, a wrong one. You remember that tun-

76

nel we dug under Russian HQ, chockablock with listening devices? That's where they caught him. Like a bloody mouse. They caught him red-handed and shot him as he tried to get back. There was an awful row, and it got into the papers. There were questions asked in the House. Where were you then, still in Italy? Waiting for a party nomination? Anyway, it was plainly my fault. He was doing what I told him to do, monitoring some devices, servicing others, when it wasn't safe. I had to get out of the service. In mid-career. Just when this girl had her baby. A bit tricky. Jess was in Berlin with me, of course, with Calvert, who was two. So I told Jess, who had some idea of what was going on, and she agreed to take the child—the mother couldn't manage on her own, away from her family, and she couldn't very well go back to the East with a brand-new baby and expect them not to ask questions. He's turned out a clever lad, Stephen. Jess was pretty fond of him, except she maintained he was sly. She adored Calvert, but she was fond of Stephen too. Except for his being sly. I don't know what I'd have done if she hadn't taken me back."

Anthony was duly surprised at the story, but it explained a good deal about Peter Wilson that had hitherto bewildered him. Then his thoughts reverted to his own affairs. "Never know what you're getting with children, do you. I could have sworn Gwen and Reggie were kind and decent women, just as I could have sworn that I was an old kind father whose frank heart gave all away. They're not, I'm not. We have to make an art of our necessities, Peter."

"I was lucky—I came back here, you sold me Clum, and I went into sheep farming." Peter became anxious. "By the way, no need to tell the boys. Calvert knows he's Jess's, Stephen knows he's adopted but not that he's mine."

"They get on, I suppose."

"Oh yes. I was glad to do it, you see. I've always been fascinated by the Germans." Peter launched into more confession. He might as well air the truth. Anthony might even explain it to him. His family used to take summer holidays in Germany in the mid-thirties, he said. There was a specially good exchange rate for travellers with useful foreign currencies, and Peter's father, who was a schoolmaster, could afford to take his family there in a battered car. One summer day they found themselves in Nuremburg. "Lovely old city, medieval churches, narrow alleys to explore. We knew nothing of the Nuremburg rallies. My parents must have been very naïve. Anyway, we were driving out of the town in the evening when one of those vast gatherings disbanded, and the car, all by itself—I suppose there wasn't much traffic in those days—met the Nazi horde, the Hitlerjugend, the Storm Troopers—the lot—all pouring out of the stadium. Thousands of large blond young men in brown, very tanned and fit, all carrying flags and Roman standards, the whole shooting match, including torches of pitch pine. Thousands and thousands of them poured past and we sat in our little car peering out wondering what in hell was going on. A poor little English family with silly little narrow ways and prejudices swept away into this glorious . . . Of course we didn't know. Did anyone know? At that moment I longed to be one of them—brown and fit and gloriously flag waving and somehow wonderfully free. I was just as taken in as they were. They were my mental age—fifteen."

"And what has that to do with Stephen?"

Peter thought. "I could never forget being so bloody frightened by all those big strong youths streaming out of the stadium, and yet wanting to be one of them. When the fighting was over, you understand, I just felt so damned sorry."

"And Stephen was to make amends."

"Or I was to make amends. It seems foolish now. I often think about it."

"You ought to tell him that you're his father."

"Would he care? I doubt it. He's making his own way very well. A good architect, well thought of in the profession, plenty of work. In fact you probably know, Gwen and Reggie have called him in to talk about doing up the hall."

"That's the first good sense they've shown since I began this business."

"Clum is to go to Calvert, of course. And Calvert got Jess's money. Jess was not so magnanimous as to leave any to my bastard."

"Stephen didn't ask about that?"

"I told him that Jess wanted to set Calvert up in farming. Stephen had his profession, you see. I said we'd agreed, Jess and I, that I'd leave him something. He didn't seem to care."

"He's not married, is he?"

"No. I thought at one time he was keen on Delia."

At this Anthony looked out of the window.

There was a long silence and then he said he regretted letting Clum go at one time, but now he was glad, because it was going to escape the clutches of his elder daughters. He stared into the small front garden with its row of Michaelmas daisies against the stone wall and the view of the abbey ruins over it. "When I remember how nearly I lost Delia . . . Gwennie's been making my life as miserable as she knows how, and all in the name of good sense. One of her themes is that Delia isn't mine."

"Christ's sake! Whose does Gwen think she is?"

"Why, yours."

"Mine?"

"Dear Heaven, let me not be mad." Anthony bowed his head.

Peter had blushed an extraordinary mottled red. Even his pale wrinkled neck was turning red. The red of his cheeks was submerged in the red of the blush.

Anthony stared at him. "If Delia were not mine, there would be more for Gwen and Reggie. I thought a blood sampling might satisfy them. Always provided we belong to different blood groups, you and I. Or is it the DNA they look at nowadays? Either one, if you'd con-sent." He twisted the dog leads in his hands till they became a muddle of leather. He said that he had to protect Delia. If it was not too late, understood. He would go to law if necessary. He wanted to cancel the transfer of the estate, which had gone badly wrong, but he understood that your word was your bond in this sort of thing. It would be a hell of a business to cancel everything and start over again.

He sounded confused. Listening, Peter remembered that he had told Alice of his one-time passion for Esmé. Surely, surely, Alice had not passed that on to Gwen. Where had Gwen got her information if not from Alice? Damn Alice! Damn her arrogance! "You can sample whatever you like. You'll have to get a sample of Delia's blood too, won't you. To match with yours. Or mine. How will she take that? And Esmé? We can all go together."

"I'm not surprised you're bitter." Anthony spoke mildly. "If I were you, I would be angry. Was I really so bad a father? Did I teach them to behave like this? I was too hard on Delia. She did nothing wrong that I can remember now. Do you know what she did wrong?"

"I did happen to hear . . ."

"Anyway, she's left. She's over in some caravan park near the Piercys. She won't speak to us. Why should she? We're moving out of the hall. Could you put us up, by the way? I don't like hotels."

"My dear man!" Then Peter remembered something. "I should tell you that Alice is joining us. I don't know how Esmé will like being with her. I wish Alice weren't coming. She's a tattletale."

"Alice? Oh, quite unreliable."

"*Is* she? I didn't know that." He started to explain apologetically that Alice could not stay on in York because Gwen had already sold her house, and she refused to move into the hall as Gwen wanted. She was going to book herself into Mrs. Fraser's in the village for a day or two, but Calvert ran into her on the street and invited her to Clum. He wanted to spare her the embarrassment of showing herself in Hartland after all those years. "I suppose she'll go back to New York eventually. But meantime she's become concerned over Delia. She seems to think that theirs is a particularly poignant relationship. I can't really understand it. What has Alice to do with Delia? Why doesn't she look after her own daughters? She thinks Delia must be encouraged. You know," he added lamely, with an incoherent anger, "I think Alice must have said something about that time when Esmé wanted an abortion. Gwen brought it up when she had no right to do so. I'd no idea she knew."

Anthony appeared to listen, but his thoughts had leapt on. "I tried to encourage Delia about her work and her response was to tear it up. Why was that?" He started to hum like a kettle of heating water. "Why was that?" He recollected his surroundings. "Women find other people's daughters easier than their own. Esmé can't even find Delia, let alone help her. She's hiding from us. Meanwhile, Gwen and Reggie are right under Alice's nose. If it's as you say and they want her to live with them in the hall, that shows how much they want to control her. They're taking their revenge. The images of revolt and flying off," he pondered. With his father dying in the war, he'd had no one to rebel against—his mother gave him his head. A clever woman. He had no need to rebel. It was different with his elder daughters. "Alice does nothing to curb Reggie and Gwen. You'd think she'd say something. She was never vengeful. Not her style. Just very bloody-minded. Keen on her own way." He resumed his humming. Then,

80

"They're putting right the wrongs of the ages, wouldn't you say. They're repairing and restoring what I neglected because I'm not fond of change for its own sake. Are you? They think they're giving order to chaos. And it's all going wrong. I'm glad of it. My years as a backbencher taught me that improvements in the long run are only ten percent successful. We'd better all go down than submit to improvements like theirs. And these are Alice's daughters! What did Alice do to them to make them the way they are?"

"They *chose* to be themselves. And the divorce must have hurt them. Jess used to say that divorce is hell on children. That's why she stuck with me, I suppose. Did you get what I said about the time Esmé wanted an abortion? Suppose Delia came to hear of that?"

"No, no. She knows nothing about that. And silly little Esmé had a girl like Delia!" He noticed the shock on Peter's face. "Unless she's yours."

"Don't be a fool."

"We have to prove it to Gwen's satisfaction. What corruption!"

Peter said something about Stephen and how he would bring some sense into the negotiations, but Anthony was not listening closely.

"Tell Stephen he is yours, or I will."

"Why should you?"

"In case he has his mind set on Delia, and she's his sister."

"What are you saying?"

"No. I'm going mad. She's fond of William Piercy. Meantime I don't know who the hell that is at the hedge, but he seems to have something to ask you. Rough-looking creature, hippy type. Tell me if you want any help with him. I can't come if Alice is to be here. Not nice for Esmé."

"I thought they got on." Peter saw the stranger come into the garden through the iron gate. He was neatly dressed and had moustaches like Caractacus and gingery hair in a ponytail. Faintly old-fashioned. Calvert wore cropped hair and a gold earring. Ah, now Peter recognised him—it was Tom Charlton wearing an unusually pious look, the fellow who worked for the Piercys on the caravan site, not a bad fellow at all.

Tom had been looking for Anthony at the hall, and the housekeeper had sent him on to Clum. He had come to introduce himself and discover more of what was going on. He would write something about it, a discreet article, a short story. It needed that sort of order put on it. It disturbed him as it was, all bits and pieces.

"Alice and Esmé get on," observed Anthony. "But it is not natural. I think they sacrifice something of themselves for the sake of getting on. There are some things you cannot ask. I do not know where Esmé and I can lay our heads, unless in some dreadful inn. I wonder if my old keeper can put us up. Oh, but he's being turfed out and put in Tufts Cottage, and it needs so much work—work that I never saw to." He groaned in agony. "Well, there's Sally Ayton, Sally and George Ayton. I'll ask them."

"Why not the Piercys," Peter said. "Or the Gowers. Or the Chambers. There's plenty of people will put you up. Friends."

"I can't ask them. My friends will despise my daughters. Imagine them on the telephone talking about the Quondams, how he was so high and mighty, how he neglected his girls, and how they got their revenge, but perhaps went too far. I'll ask Sally and George Ayton. They'll look after us. We'll get decorators out from York to finish Akeld, and move in."

Peter Wilson's gift of a confession had made Anthony forget himself. His thoughts returned to his old interests. He called Tom Charlton's attention to a dark line running down the hillside, beyond the gulley, and the next line twenty or thirty yards to the right, and the one at the same distance further along. A whole series. What did Tom think they were?

Tom at first could not see what the old man meant. Then he saw the faint marks on the old pasture in its winter dormancy, brought into focus by the slanting light. "That's not rig and furrow, is it?"

Anthony was pleased. "No, rig and furrow show the medieval field system. Those are Celtic fields, worked in different manner, and divided up before the Angles and the Saxons came, I am not sure how, perhaps with an earthen wall or a low line of stones that have sunk, which would account for the darkness of the marking. They're not on any of the estate maps as such. So—Roman-British, or earlier, half or three quarters of an acre each. Two or three thousand years old. Our present ploughland would have been woods and moor, but the hillside would have been cleared, and it would have been drained by the fall of the land so a span of oxen could plough one of those fields in a couple of days. I must go over one day and see if I can find traces of boundary."

Tom stared at the hillside and saw nothing much.

"Now these are the former commons we're walking over.

> The law locks up the man or woman
> Who steals the goose from off the common
> But lets the greater villain loose
> Who steals the common off the goose

—in this case, Henry Quondam." He halted and put out a hand to halt Tom too. They looked at the huge house in front of them. "We may be getting our come-uppance now."

Tom waited, but Anthony took himself and the hall for granted. It did not occur to him that others might expect to hear some justification of himself and his possessions. His thoughts flowed one into the other, and the listener had a hard time finding the connection. Now he went on to tell of a clergyman called Clutter who wrote a history of Hartland and its environs in 1820 and praised the munificence of the Quondam of those days for letting the villagers graze their animals in the parkland they were walking over. "He didn't say that only thirty years earlier the land was commons. It belonged to the villagers, not John Quondam. The villagers were illiterate, you see. No one knows what they said, because they didn't write it down. And the parson didn't write it down either. Parson Clutter owed them nothing. Whereas he owed his living to John Quondam. The hall is a mirage, you see, Tom. Just below us in the mid–eighteenth century someone found the site of a Roman villa, and up on the slopes opposite, see those little terraces, shelves really, along the side of the bank, those are strip lynchets, early fields that the Roman master must have continued to cultivate." He pointed them out. "The countryside is full of mysteries. Another thing Clutter mentioned was the existence of a mill over at Howden, a mile or two from here. The village there has died out. But in Clutter's day you could still see the millrace up on the part they called the Stripe, and though I've looked for it, I haven't found it. But it was never tillage except for a year or two in the war, and it isn't tillage now, and I think I must have been looking in the wrong part. If you're interested, we could go there and look again. Will you come? One day soon I'll write up my village history." He was pleased at Tom's interest. "So you want to know the details of the transfer of the hall. Well, there is a time to give things up. The Emperor Charles the Fifth went to Granada and began building himself a great solemn place to retire to near the Alhambra. He was going to be a monk. The Holy Roman Empire could take a different course when he left it. One of my daughters says I'm infirm and have never been well. The other says I have never been other than rash and now I am wayward. You will decide for yourself, Tom. I'm leaving my little empire and retiring to my monastery, though with my wife." He had yet to consider Peter Wilson's confession. He had not much to put up with. He would be the pattern of patience. What had he done? Nothing! But Delia had done nothing either, and look how he'd treated her.

At the garden entry to the hall he remembered what they had come for. "I'm not going into the hall. There'll be complaints. My shoes are muddy." Again this went down perfectly well. He had not betrayed anything of the tremendous row with Gwen, and if he missed his murdered dogs, no one would know. He repeated to Tom, "Perhaps you should ask my daughters about the transfer before you talk to me. You'll find Mrs. Bowers and Mrs. Smith in the hall," and he started back in the direction of the Aytons', thinking that he had to settle the immediate future. It would be a comfort to talk to George and Sally. When he was a younger man he had gone to Ithaca and built himself a hut out of driftwood on the beach and lived there for months. The villagers had brought him olives and bread and wine. He now saw himself living alone in a hut with a dog, like Robinson Crusoe, when all had left him. But Esmé would not like that kind of life. And he was too old to live rough. The attraction of doing so only slipped across his mind now and then like a small furred wild animal, barely identified.

6

Alice heard of Delia's departure from the hall with infinite pity. She heard of it through Reggie, who rang from Harrogate, where she was putting her house on the market. The Smiths had lived there fourteen years and the dispersal of such hopeful objects as tennis racquets in need of string, dog baskets in need of a dog, ball gowns in need of a ball, and keys in need of a lock brought out Reggie's latent spite. Why should she be stuck with such work when a move to Quondam Hall might bankrupt them and they might need hopeful things to sell or mend? Reggie was used to being decisive, but she was always busy with charitable committees and a social life that was supposed to augment and glorify Jeremy's work at Sotheby's, so her teeth were continually put on edge. And the moment that the attic and cellar were bare, the house touched up with paint, the floors and furniture waxed, the curtains washed and the windows cleaned, the silver polished and put on display, and flowers arranged, and above all, now that the house was tidy all day, customers tramped through so consistently that Reggie was half-dead with exhaustion and the hypocrisy of presenting a smiling face to the world. She therefore let fly about Delia. Delia was downright selfish; she deserved what had been coming to her for a long time. She was also caustic about Gwen. Alice realised that Reggie was afraid that Gwen would nibble at her portion of the estate and that she would be left with less than half. As Reggie was on duty keeping the house on show, she wanted her mother to make sure of her full share. Delia looked good and innocent in comparison, but Alice trembled with willingness to love her, with abandon, extravagantly, energetically, not just in homage to virtue.

Why Delia moved her to such would-be passion was puzzling. Injustice is evil, but the injustice to Delia could be remedied by Esmé, who would surely give her a decent sum to live on to compensate for the loss of one third of the hall and estate (what were they worth, after all, on the open market?). Gwen and Reggie might have been all in all to Alice if they hadn't been so unattractive, and if their unattractiveness hadn't been partly her fault. She was growing weary of the burden of their unpleasantness. Poor Delia! She might have ended before she began, if her young mother had succeeded in having her way. How strange it was that Gwen and Reggie, who'd been lavished with affection, were nasty, while Delia, who'd been neglected, was sweetness and light. Unsuccessful with her own daughters, Alice felt she might help Delia, who was in need of help. But where exactly was Delia? Alice went to Quondam Hall to find out.

So driving into the hall after her visit to Akeld, Esmé met Alice, who was driving out. They stopped their cars next to each other, and the population of Hartland took note. In vain did Esmé tell herself that the hall was no longer hers; in vain did Alice remember that she was only a visitor and her real life lay elsewhere. The village was watching Anthony Quondam's two wives and comparing them and coming to conclusions about Anthony as a husband, and laughing, laughing, laughing. This was the real stuff of village life, providing human interest in a thick slab of cake. Every nuance of the encounter would be laid under the general scrutiny and seriously as well as comically debated before passing into legend, as such incidents had been from the beginning of time. Far more interesting, and far more pleasurable, and far more moral, than videos or the telly or books, the meeting struck everyone as the real thing, denied them for so long by the high walls of the hall.

The wives lowered their car windows to each other. Esmé explained what she had been doing. Alice replied with expressions of amazement. Delia couldn't be found? Weird. She was hiding? Impossible. Alice laughed sweetly. Esmé nodded and smiled. So no one could have been more difficult than Reggie and Gwen? Surely not. Who would have believed it?

Esmé found Alice overpowering. She wished to tell her that Delia had never been difficult, while she remembered with horror the first time she met Reggie and Gwen, hostile contemporaries, when she had just married their father. Difficult girls they'd always been, according to Anthony. Everyone who came to the hall told her the same, offering the information as a warning and looking at her compassionately. However, if she said now, "I know," she would have been discourteous and gone against her conscience, while Alice would break in and declare, "That's what I'm saying!" as if Esmé were contradicting. A maddening habit. To avoid trouble, she simply said, "We'll be at the Aytons'."

"You're leaving the hall? Akeld is ready? No? Then why not stay?"

Esmé felt she was strangling. "We do not wish it."

"Oh. Very well. Surely there is room at the hall? Gwennie and Reggie will be very hurt if you don't stay there. Everyone will think they're driving you out."

Driving her out? Esmé looked for irony in Alice's face and saw none. She said stiffly, "That is kind, but we prefer to stay with the Aytons for a little while."

"Oh, very well." Alice looked mystified. But she had not run to the end of good advice. "Then why don't you leave Delia alone if you're leaving the hall? There's no need to bother her, is there? I strongly advise you to leave her and let her seek you out in good time."

Esmé nodded. She was of course leaving Delia alone and had as good as said so. In accordance with her usual practice, she had not said so in as many words because that would have meant expressing an opinion, which would have meant having to justify herself. And if Alice was completely out of touch with what was going on, shouting through car windows in public was not the best way to enlighten her. Even if they met face to face, though, she knew Alice would ignore what she said and proceed to state the contrary. So Esmé made her statement then for want of a better time. "I would like to make sure that Delia gets her share of the hall."

"But Anthony has disinherited her!"

"That is one way of putting it. I would not put it like that. He now regrets he lost his temper. As far as he is concerned, she has every right to her share of the hall." Alice began to speak, but Esmé was determined not to give way. "Your daughters seem to believe that she is not Anthony's and therefore has no right anyway to her share. We are arranging a DNA analysis."

"Esmé! How appalling! They didn't tell me that!" Alice instantly wept the hot remorseful tears of a Magdalene. She tried to speak, but her voice drowned in sobs. She remembered clearly what Reggie had said to her on the subject months ago. It was one thing to repeat an interesting rumour. It was quite another to act on it as if it were the truth. Or was she herself the gossip who had passed on this rumour? Had she voiced what she privately thought? The tears had burst out spontaneously with a life of their own, as if they were ashamed of her.

"They may have thought you knew," Esmé said, looking shyly at the tears on the red face.

"She *is* Anthony's daughter, isn't she, Esmé?"

Esmé felt faint. "That is quite enough!"

Her anger surprised Alice, who had never got anything out of Esmé in the past but softness and honey. And yet she did not believe her. Her own boldness had only made Esmé defend herself, not necessarily with the truth. "I shouldn't have asked that."

"No, you should not."

"People don't want to believe that an old man can have such a perfect daughter. That's how such rumours start. Now I've made *you* cry, Esmé."

Esmé shook her head. She could not speak. She wiped her eyes in the car mirror.

"Does Delia know of this rumour, Esmé? I'll see that she knows of it. It's better if she's forewarned." Esmé shook her head again. Alice's moral generosity was as frightful as her outspokenness. "I am very sorry about this, Esmé. How difficult for you. But you have Akeld to look forward to, don't you. Akeld was always the Quondams' bolt-hole." Alice had recovered herself, but now she fell headlong into laughter. Knowledge of the inglorious past had been a great comfort to Alice during her marriage.

For Esmé, ignorance had always been a comfort. She noted the laughter with distaste, not understanding it, and murmured that she knew as much of that as she wished.

A plumber's van then appeared seeking access to the hall, and the cars were forced to move in their opposite directions to let it through. Esmé escaped to Delia's barn feeling battered. On the other hand she felt some sympathy for Alice, who one day soon would discover what monsters her daughters were. Esmé dreaded that day, because in spite of the many difficulties she created, Alice was a bulwark against the wickedness of the world.

Alice found Delia by the simple method of driving to the caravans after dark and walking to the one with a lighted interior. She knocked and Delia opened immediately. She had been expecting William, who was due back from Leeds.

"It's Alice. Alice Quondam. It's years since we met. You were twelve. You probably don't remember me. Alice Quondam, no relation. Or a relation with no name. You don't have to talk to me, Delia dear, but I've been dreadfully worried about you." Sinking in the mud below the door, Alice looked up into the dazzle of the doorway with a radiant, unresentful smile.

Delia didn't believe her. Her happiness in the caravan depended upon being left alone in it. Who was Alice Quondam anyway, to be worried about her? But in the past she had respected the idea of Alice, who had so cleverly moved away to make her own life. Not only had she moved away, but she'd proved herself, studied retailing, opened a shop in Pimlico selling first-class kitchen equipment just when interest in food was mounting with the salaries to gratify it, become a successful businesswoman in London, and then flown off to New York to become even more successful. Rich, glamorous Alice, as Delia remembered her nine or ten years ago, smiling and scented and wearing a wonderful leather coat like a character in early German cinema. Older but still daunting, Alice stood trim and upright in black polished cavalry boots, now unfortunately caked with mud, and a long mulberry-coloured raincoat, very well cut, with lots of silver buttons. A black gloved hand kept in place a very large soft leather bag on her shoulder. The only item in her appearance not in place was her white hair, which blew disarmingly round her face. The face was scrubbed, red-cheeked, beaming. The eyes were kind and brown. Delia reluctantly invited her in.

"I've been terribly distressed by Anthony's treatment of you," Alice said, settling herself on one of the two hard chairs drawn up to the collapsible table. She drew off her gloves, releasing a smell of marvellous scent. The cold, stuffy caravan began to smell marvellous too. Underneath, though, from the laden shoulder bag, there also began to manifest itself a pungent and incongruous smell of pâté and olives and goat's cheese.

Delia, who was wearing old and dirty jeans and one of William's shirts, was embarrassed. "You shouldn't worry about me."

"No. Dear Delia, I don't pardon what Anthony has done. That's for you to do. But it was untypical, wouldn't you say?"

"I don't know about that." She repeated, for its shock value, the phrase she'd used to William: "I find my father *pretty comic.* A dear man, everyone loves him. He doesn't belong in the real world. He has no idea of what I'm trying to do. He thinks he does, he thinks he can see me clearly because I'm his daughter. He's so old. It's a relief just to be here."

"Yes. You are on your own, free as a bird." Alice looked round at the caravan and found it disgusting. Her eyes came to rest on the solitary teacup and she looked away in pity. "Delia, you simply made no attempt to please him, isn't that it? Unlike Gwennie or Reggie, who knew what they were supposed to say, and said it—'Daddy! We adore you more than anyone in the world!' Rather silly for women with husbands and children."

"He can believe them if he wants. Why shouldn't he believe his own children! What he asked was reasonable, and *I* said something reasonable back, I can't remember what, and he reasonably told me to get out. We were both of us tremendously reasonable. But you see, Alice, as far as I'm concerned, he's old and confused. He thinks I'm glorious youth, or something of the sort. We haven't a thing in common. I mean, I've often thought that I could easily be someone else's daughter. I gather there's a rumour about it. Mother was always running around with other men. Do you know that she tried to abort me?"

"She was very young," Alice said earnestly, completely taken aback.

"Oh, you know about that. The funny thing is that the abortion scare and the illegitimacy scare have made me much fonder of Esmé, and of my father too. I should say, 'of Anthony.'" Delia laughed merrily.

Alice mumbled something about the perpetual unreality of relations. She was for once at a loss. The situation had completely changed. To take hold, she opened the mysteriously smelly shoulder bag and it disgorged a bottle of burgundy, some bread rolls smelling still of the oven, pâté, cheese, a twist of olives, and a bag of Cox's orange pippins. "I hope you haven't dined?" she asked politely, with a look at Delia's extreme thinness.

Delia believed she had a good head for drink. On her third glass of wine she boldly got out her secret sketches and laid them out against the wall at the back of a bunk, and put on the floor in front of a bunk a small oil painting. She had apparently been busy on scenes from a battlefield; the dead and wounded had been carted away and only the bombed and blasted land was evidence of what had taken place. In one sketch, however, there was a single running figure, male or female, tearing down a trail to a corner. Alice assumed that the landscape was an interior one, it was so bleak. She said in a fright, "Oh! Oh! Delia, these are strong!"

The artist stood back and frowned. She had been trying for the grainy brown desolation of Matthew Brady's photos of the Civil War, she explained, the bareness, the shock bareness. They were of the clear-felling at Akeld. Oh, didn't Alice know?—Gwen had ordered the oaks felled. A terrific scene, really, those enormous bodies flat at last. Yes, they had curious shapes, some of them, *vestigial* was the word. Oaks last forever, even when they look pollarded and just a few twigs stick out, like fingers from shoulders; if leaves keep coming, the oaks survive, and they were very extraordinary to look at, as if they were having parties in the fields, clumped together. It was the money for the timber Gwen was after. Seasoned oak fetched huge prices. Delia knew because a friend of hers was a furniture designer and maker. Yes, the oil was quite a success, she was fairly pleased with that. Would Alice choose one of the sketches as a gift from her?

"Oh! Oh! How could she order them felled? How could she do it?"

"For the hall. Every cottage in Hartland is up for sale. They've sold Adriaen de Vries's fighting horses to the Getty."

"They frighten me," Alice said, referring to the artwork.

"I know."

Alice realised that Delia thought she meant Gwen and Reggie.

"Alice . . ." Pause. "Alice, I hate to say this, but the painter is penniless. Can you lend me some money?"

Alice immediately emptied her wallet and laid five twenty-pound bank notes on the table. She then got out her cheque-book and wrote Delia a cheque for two hundred pounds. There was more where that came from, she said. She had plenty of money in a local bank account, and she intended to transfer a lump sum soon from the Chase Manhattan; her New York shop had made her a woman of means. Everyone wanted the best pots and pans in her kitchen. The more expensive the better. Good pots and pans meant you knew what was important. She had no intention of supporting Gwen and Reggie's schemes for the hall. She would rather support a decent painter. Delia also appeared to have been done out of her share of Anthony's estate. She should litigate.

Then she picked out the best of the sketches for herself.

Delia blushed.

"Litigate!" cried Alice. Delia blushed even more. "Why not come back with me to New York after Christmas? We can find you a loft in Soho!" She burst into a eulogy of the view over Central Park from her apartment in the wintertime with the trees stuck like antlers through the peeled bald skin of the landscape, tiny lights netted among bare branches; the lights of cars, yellow-bright headlights, red brake lights; traffic lights red and green and yellow luminosities winking as the traffic surged and crawled; towers of banked illuminations, like ocean liners in the far distance. Then on the hard, cold streets the puddles and pot-holes, the terrible raddled faces, the bright terrible faces, the bright shiny nylon clothes, the waste of boards and metal and frozen earth where down-and-out men, alcoholics, druggies, lost souls, in thick dirty dark wrappings warmed themselves over buckets of fire.

The little shops with their funny brilliant clothes, the department stores all glitter and cleverness and appeal to the purse. Dangerous, exciting, vulgar city. A far cry from the North Riding.

Delia smiled and looked again at her sketches.

"You could do with a good dose of vulgarity, Delia."

"Oh Alice."

"That bloody hall."

"Yes. Mother ran away from it once."

"Well, you see?"

"There was a man, too. I don't know who. My McEachnie grandfather brought her back. Mum's father. I seem to remember some of the fuss."

"You see? She was running away from the house." Poor, poor little Esmé, Alice thought with approval. "Have you a boyfriend, Delia?"

"I'm going to marry William Piercy, I think. We've been together for several years off and on. There was a guy in London I used to see. . . . But no, probably I'll marry William. If I marry anyone."

Alice poured herself the last glass. "We have to safeguard your rights. Tomorrow afternoon, Delia, we are meeting to discuss the future of the hall, and I want you to come. Your presence will signify that you are standing up for yourself before the plans are laid in concrete. You have to make known your point of view. Gwen and Reggie will be there, and I will be there—though I have no right to be—and I hope that Anthony can be persuaded to come, and Esmé, and Stephen Wilson, with his projections—he's handling the money side, did you know that? We'll hear what must be done sooner and what later, and how the money will be raised to cover the costs, and the number of visitors a year who can be attracted, and what you must do to get a grant."

"If you think it's a good idea, I'll come."

"Everyone will be delighted." Alice got up to go and impulsively kissed Delia more readily than she ever kissed her own daughters or grandchildren, and received a more ready response from Delia than ever from them. Or so it seemed, as they hugged. Now why was that, Alice asked herself as they drew apart, why hadn't she loved her daughters freely and been loved back? Was it because she had always been frank about Anthony to the girls, believing that if she disguised his faults they would never learn the truth about human nature? Could she have been spiteful, unwittingly? Could they have picked up some habit of scepticism and looked at her as coldly as she looked at Anthony?

"I believe you're coming for your father's sake," Alice said fondly. "You're very close to him, aren't you? Closer than to your mother? I was very much in love with him at the beginning of my marriage, before it went sour. We lived together before the wedding, I don't suppose you knew that. He was perfectly splendid. I adored him."

She spoke as if throwing money about. It was surprising to see Delia suddenly in tears. "I'll give Stephen Wilson and Gwen due notice that you're coming tomorrow." She pretended not to see the tears, half-jealous, half-ashamed of the ease with which she had provoked this display of emotion, but above all glad that at least some of her tenderness for Delia had its answer.

Tom Charlton tidied his hair by freeing it from its elastic band, shaking his head vigorously, then knotting it securely and smoothly into the band again. He then flicked his moustaches and advanced into the old service wing of the hall in search of Mr. Quondam's elder daughters, whom he'd never met. He knew that they were much older than Delia and that their married names were Mrs. Bowers and Mrs. Smith, but that was about all he knew. The mystery attracted him. He knew women better than men, having been brought up by them. His father had been a master mariner, born in Whitby and practising his trade from Humberside and Tyneside, where Tom's mother came from. He'd been lost at sea when Tom was six years old. Thereafter his mother had gone back to Newcastle and set up house with a younger sister, Jenny, who looked after Tom and his two elder sisters while Mrs. Charlton herself went back to teaching. She eventually became the headmistress of a big school for girls in the city.

Far from missing his father, Tom had enjoyed being the only male in the house. As the youngest child, he'd picked up what he now saw as feminine virtues—mercy instead of justice, mildness instead of pushiness, intuitive understanding instead of intellectual analysis. He got on well with his mother, who had now retired, and his sisters, one of whom had married a forester in Cumbria and ran a plant centre; the other worked for Wedgwood as a designer and lived in the Midlands. He went to stay with each of them two or three times a year. Women were easier to talk to, had less to prove, more to imagine, were simply better at living, than men. Marriage therefore seemed a perfectly delightful state to enter into. But his wife did not see the marriage in the same light. She was terribly unhappy. After a year, she left him for someone else. He resigned from his job as a traffic coordinator, sold his house and his beloved motorbike, cleared out, and wandered from one city to another taking a job for a month at a time and then leaving. He thought his life was destroyed. Then he discovered nature and Piercy Castle.

The news that the transfer of Quondam Hall to the three daughters had gone badly wrong struck him at first as implausible. Delia seemed an easy and responsible woman. Probably her sisters were easy and responsible too. Old Mr. Quondam must have alienated them. He appeared to have alienated Delia, though she did not say so. And Tom gathered from talking to Esmé that the elder sisters were getting into a lot of trouble, though she did not say so either. It was the subject of much interest in the pubs, but pub talk was nauseating, so nauseating that the honourable thing appeared plain: he would contrive to meet old Mr. Quondam and ask for the whole story with its details so that he could write about them in a free-lance newspaper article. In return he would ask Mr. Quondam if he could be of service to him.

Tom saw nothing odd in the idea of asking barefaced questions. And to be sure, Mr. Quondam proved most open and approachable. But the idea of asking him about the transfer cock-up turned out to be only theoretically possible. It might be different with the women. Women, he theorized, had less variety than men, because they had less power and less experience. He had, for example, never met any man like Anthony Quondam.

He thought he would approach Mrs. Bowers and Mrs. Smith with a plain north-countryman's directness. But as he advanced into the cold dark recesses of the disused wing, he heard a man and a woman laughing in the distance, and was dismayed. Old Anthony Quondam would not laugh so recklessly. He would have more dignity, more sense of solemn occasion, more sense of Tom. This laughter fell like a curtain in a theatre, between stage world and reality. Tom, caught in his soliloquy, felt mocked. Still, he was as good as any man alive; he advanced doggedly into a big room, stone cold, musty, damp, with a huge fireplace and stone flags on the floor and a lantern tower extending up through the ceiling and roof to let fumes out and air and light in. Under this light sat Gwen Bowers and Stephen Wilson at a pine table in a balloon of noise and intimacy. A dusty wine bottle, its cork drawn, stood before them, and two wine glasses half-full. She had her hand on his arm as they chortled, a thin tall woman in glasses, lots of teeth, and a man in a natty blue blazer with silver buttons, teeth just as numerous but straighter, head balding on the crown where there wasn't a gingery fringe of light feathery hair, pink cheeks, a signet ring on his little finger. Side by side they sat, like strange magistrates.

"Pardon me," said Tom, prepared to launch into a series of questions. Then he thought better of it and turned round and went out of the room and up the stairs to the library, where he started examining the books.

It was a well-dimensioned room with a plain dentil cornice, the bookcases set in under it, and three massive sash windows. There were thousands of books here, some in elaborate leather-bound eighteenth-century sets, some in plain nineteenth-century sombre style, some newish, in coloured bindings. And there were pamphlets and leaflets and folders wedged among them here and there. Tom pulled out a pamphlet printed in early nineteenth-century lettering, titled *An Essay on the Roman Remains at Aldborough in the County of Yorkshire*, by a clergyman resident in that parish. The first paragraph described where Aldborough was. Tom had barely begun on the second when Gwen Bowers and Stephen Wilson walked in. "Right, then!" Tom declared, replacing the pamphlet and realising that this was the first private library he had ever been in and that he therefore was trespassing.

Gwen immediately understood. The library had been new to her as an adult too, and she too had been a freshman undergraduate wandering through a university library like Eve in Eden. She introduced herself and Stephen Wilson and asked if Mrs. Quondam hadn't sent him.

"Mr. Quondam."

"Ah."

He explained his interest in writing about the transfer.

"An article? How very much to the point! Don't you agree, Stephen? Stephen here has been using the library and has found out a great deal we didn't know. Are you good at libraries? We don't know what's here, do we, Stephen, it hasn't been catalogued for over a hundred years and then they did it badly. Yet it's essential to know what we've got, isn't it. If we knew what was here, we could no doubt fill you in admirably. As it is . . ."

"I've made several interesting discoveries just in the past week," Stephen Wilson said. "One in particular that's going to make all the difference to Quondam Hall and Hartland itself. I believe you know the youngest Quondam daughter. She's coming tomorrow afternoon, and so's her mother, Mrs. Esmé Quondam. And Mrs. Smith—Reggie—Mrs. Bowers's sister, and their mother, Mrs. Alice Quondam. We're going to talk about the actual foundation of the enterprise that's about to be launched. Perhaps you'd like to be present? At two, tomorrow, here."

"You know," said Gwen with a show of frankness, "if you want to use this library, that's all right by me. I wonder if you would be interested in a longer-term project. How about the catalogue? Have you had any experience of that sort?"

"I've worked as a cataloguer, part-time, as a student, in the university library at Newcastle. I have a B.A. degree from Newcastle, in mathematics. I'd need a computer. It would take a fair time, of course." Tom was amazed at the freedom with which Mrs. Bowers was offering him a job. (Was he right in thinking she was doing that?) "You know nothing about me," he said.

"The Piercys have told me that you were wasted on the caravan site. You've consulted their library, haven't you? Lady Piercy said that you made some excellent recommendations. She was astonished, if you don't mind my saying so."

"I was looking up the origins of their garden layout. No, I don't look like a librarian." He grinned and touched his moustaches. "I don't know what I want to look like, but I don't want to look like a librarian."

They all laughed merrily, and then Gwen said that if he wanted to work in a library, he might find things easier if he adopted the

97

uniform. She spoke with authority and kindness. With a shot at equal firmness, he asked about salary.

"We'll have to think a little before we make you an offer."

He explained that he was still managing the site over at Piercy Castle, but they had reached the back end and there was little to do.

Gwen added, "We're devising a budget for the next five years. It needs big capital to run a place like this successfully, you see, Mr. Charlton."

"Tom."

"Thank you. Tom, then." He expected her to add that her Christian name was Gwen and that the other's name was Stephen, but she didn't. Perhaps she forgot. No, don't be stupid, he told himself; she hadn't forgotten, she was a snob. And they were covering something up, something he'd happened on as he came on them in the old kitchen.

"A lot of capital is what we need," said Stephen Wilson.

"The repair bill is high. My father has neglected the house. The estate supported it, but he simply saw to what was in urgent need of repair. There was no decoration or anything of that sort. The library should be one of the first rooms to be refurbished. We're in desperate need of a cataloguer so that we have a record of the books when they are taken off the shelves and repaired, and while the redecoration goes ahead. Can you get us references from the University Librarian at Newcastle? And his telephone number?" She added that they would need a new visitors' guide and a short history of the house to send out with the publicity when the restoration was complete. He might busy himself with that as well.

At this new and unearned mark of favour, Tom was even more dubious. Did they think they'd get him cheap? How did they know he would do a good job? Or didn't they care what sort of a job he did? Perhaps it was enough for them that he had a university degree. Or were they ashamed at being found like that, laughing and a bit drunk, alone together, and were they covering up by diverting his attention to himself? Or, most likely of all, were they amateurs at the job of launching a country house on the tourist market, and did their interest in him represent floundering?

But they seemed intent on carrying him along in a great gush of enthusiasm. Stephen had turned to Gwen and was asking her if he shouldn't let Tom into the picture now. He would hear all about it tomorrow anyway. If he heard ahead of time, that would give him more opportunity to think things over and give an accurate rundown of their schemes. And Stephen leapt to a shelf and pulled out a box file. "Those books there, Tom, have to do with the history of Hartland and the vicinity. In this file here I discovered that in 1931 Anthony had certain tests carried out in Swathbeck Vale, hoping to find petroleum deposits. There are beds of shale there, and the tests were quite common in those days. They were exploring, you know, men from I.C.I. looking for cheap sources of fuel for their plant at Billingham. Well, luckily for us, perhaps, they didn't find any petroleum. Or gas. It was waiting for them under the North Sea. What they did find, though, is extremely interesting." He paused dramatically and balanced his right hand on the table so that the fingers formed the struts of a tent. He had a long, lean fine hand that the gesture showed off to perfection.

"What they found, Tom, was an eighteen-mile stretch of high-grade gravel, half a mile wide in places. There was no method of extracting it cheaply then, and of course very little road building going on, since the depression capped expenditure on roads. The Germans, with their usual foresight and energy, were busy building vast autobahns crisscrossing Germany, but people here were trapped in the parliamentary inertia. So the plans were shelved. Nowadays we have vast earth-moving machines which make such projects much more economical. And—it so happens—there's that new motorway to be introduced between the Tyne and Lincoln which will pass within a few miles of here."

He paused to let the news sink in. "I am sure you grasp the significance. No? Let's explain here a little. New roads like motorways require vast quantities of gravel for their foundation, and the nearest operative gravel pits at present are about one hundred miles away from the sector to pass nearest Hartland. So what's the situation? A new major motorway proposed within a few miles of Hartland to draw traffic off the existing motorways. A crying new need for high-quality gravel. An answer to that need—the Swathbeck Vale deposits. So we have need, and we have the means to satisfy that need."

"So we're going to get rich, are we," Tom said agreeably.

"Well, let me tell you. I was so excited that I got in touch with the original surveyors, now no less than Walkett Brewer Aggregates. It has been pretty well established over the years that the deposits are even greater than was at first supposed. They've known about the deposits all along, of course, and they were quick to take me up. We think that acting in partnership we'll get the money we're aiming for to restore the hall. Which will cost plenty, believe me. Of course we will need an up-to-date survey, but that's just a matter of routine. Walkett Brewer see no reason to hang about. We mean to apply for permission, planning consent, and so forth, and I see no problem there. We all stand to gain by the gravel extraction. That's poor tillage, they tell me, by the way, where the gravel is."

"So you'll bring prosperity to the area," Tom said.

"Absolutely."

"Can't quarrel with that."

"Exactly. Can't quarrel with that. We'll make Quondam Hall a showplace, and everyone will benefit. Mind you, we shan't change the basic nature of the village. It'll still be a lovely quiet village, but it'll be really well-off. Think of those towns in the Cotswolds—they were made lovely by wealth, the wealth of the sheep trade. You don't get good-looking towns and villages without an excellent economic substructure."

"Sounds all right," Tom said, and wished he had been making notes.

"Tom, we're going to revive the quarrying that has always been carried out in this area. The countryside here is pitted with stone quarries, as you know. Concealed, most of them. Grown over. It has been quarried for centuries. Certainly since the Romans, who built roads of local stone. There's nothing *startlingly* new in what we're proposing to do. The only thing that's really novel is the purpose of the operation, A, and, B, our modern ability to extract with machinery on a large scale."

"Well! Sounds all right." He wished he had something more brilliant to say, but the other two seemed delighted with him as he was. It was their excitement with the gravel business that had made them look as though they were plotting earlier on, he decided. He was pleased with the vindication. Nothing is worse than suspicion.

7

"Do we know why Anthony isn't here?" Stephen Wilson beamed at his four listeners. They sat in twos on benches facing him. Tom Charlton sat on one bench with Esmé, and on the bench opposite sat the sisters Gwen and Reggie. Gwen was neat and casual in blue jeans and sweater as she had been the day before; Reggie, loud and expensive in black and white checks, with gold chains hung at her neck and waist, her skirt short to display plenty of leg in opaque black tights, with black patent shoes to show off her narrow feet. When she moved, the gold chains jiggled. Stephen looked her up and down not once but several times, and she met his look each time with a half smile. Gwen saw. But Reggie was always adversarial. Everything she did was intended to rouse people to confront her. You were not permitted to ignore Reggie. Better betrayed than ignored, she maintained, and did not care who heard her.

"As a point of order, why isn't he?" Stephen pressed.

Esmé looked up meekly. "It's better not."

"Oh? In point of fact, he couldn't come?"

"He lay down to rest just now and had bad dreams. Dreams of suffocation and prisons and, oh I don't know, a church hall piled with clothes for a jumble sale. He had to sleep on them, in the dream. He was a beggar, hiding from someone or other. I couldn't make out who was chasing him. When he woke up, he was in no fit state . . ."

"He's in a rage," Reggie observed.

"We can't blame him, poor chap," said Stephen heartily. "My father gets like that. Has bad dreams. And so he might. You agree? Some people should have bad dreams."

There was a silence. "We all should," said Tom.

Gwen laughed merrily.

"He remembers about the war in his dreams—the shellfire and the bodies mostly." Esmé spoke softly and sadly.

Gwen cleared her throat and wiped her glasses.

Reggie stared over Tom's head. "If he wants to injure himself, we can't stop him. It may do him good. It may teach him a lesson."

"What lesson?" When Tom spoke, Reggie lowered her gaze and met Tom's eyes and looked away again.

"Mother's late," said Gwen.

"He said he would not open his mouth, so there was no point in his coming." Esmé hated having to explain.

"He's nursing his rage," said Gwen.

"He's being very patient!"

Stephen turned briskly to the passage leading to the buttery and pantry and suggested a tour before Alice turned up—"If we want to wait for her, that is?"—to which the sisters replied that they did. The three of them set off down the passage.

"It was the little mittens and little socks that disturbed him, in the dream. The clothes in the church hall for some jumble sale." Esmé looked at Tom and spoke in a candid voice.

"Oh?" Tom tried hard to imagine the old man on the piles of worn clothing in the dream, and to realise what it was like to be Esmé, a woman roughly the same age as her stepdaughters. All they had in common was their relationship to the old man, who was not like any of them.

"Why are we meeting here? I hate this part of the house." Esmé looked around in distress. Most of the old kitchen quarters, where they now were, had been abandoned in the heyday of Anthony's mother. Widowed and free to do as she wished, she tried to make some kind of a nest for herself and her boy, and the kitchens wouldn't yield. So she made another kitchen and a breakfast room out of the old gun room upstairs. That was in the twenties. A success in its day, the updating itself now looked dismal. The ancient kitchens on the other hand had gained some glamour from their impracticality.

Stephen and the two sisters presently returned. "You could have an excellent restaurant space here," he was saying, waving a hand like a salesman. "We'll strip off that lime and wash render and expose the old bricks, which are very handsome—I've chipped some of the render off in the wine cellar and you have these lovely handmade bricks underneath. People in London would give a fine penny for them. At the moment, moisture is seeping in behind patches of cement which Anthony must have had applied in the thirties to some of the worst places—which have of course deteriorated further. It was a most unsatisfactory method of repair but we didn't know it then."

"What *we* is this, then?"

They looked at Tom in surprise. "Ha-ha! A way of speaking. On behalf of the fraternity." Stephen smiled at Reggie before smiling at Tom. Reggie laughed, Tom did not. He scowled at the navy blazer with silver buttons. "There may be problems with ventilation," Stephen added.

"Well, look who's here," Reggie said in a gangster voice. Delia had appeared at a loop in the passage.

"It's so nice to see you again, darling," Esmé said, brightening. "But why have you been hiding? You used to be so sweet and open." Delia sat beside her and squeezed her hand.

Alice appeared, jingling her car keys. She heard Esmé's anguish. "Of course she was sweet, Esmé. She still is."

"What happened?" Esmé repeated, not taking her eyes off her daughter.

Alice said briskly, "You can't go on being simply sweet, can you? Sweetness is natural to the young, like complicity. We get more complicated and the sweetness goes."

"Shut up," said Esmé.

"You can't mean that, Mum."

"No, I don't mean it. Sorry, Alice."

"My fault."

Stephen had made a simple and satisfactory discovery. "I've just worked out that you're all Quondam women. I'm surrounded by Quondams! *Mirabile dictu!*" His face was rosy with social merriment.

"Jesus," said Tom.

Stephen did not relinquish his smile. "Now I was saying to Reggie and Gwen earlier, these kitchens would make excellent restaurants. You'll have a cafeteria over there, in very good style of course, and a first-class restaurant, much smaller, in the old servants' hall. The district lacks a decent restaurant, as you know, and this would be a definite draw, especially as the hall is right in the village and not miles away in a park. Now there at the entrance you'd have your other big money-maker, your shop . . ."

"You're going to be in on this, are you?" Reggie asked Delia.

"Oh, why not? What do you want me to do—run the shop? Or take tickets at the entrance? Or sell programmes and brochures? I could be a guide, or one of those nice ladies in navy with white touches and a badge to show they're authentic, holding a Ping-Pong bat with the details printed on it about the pictures and furniture that visitors like to ask about."

"Are you being snobbish?"

"Flippant, I think," said Gwen.

"No need for the sarcasm, Delia, we all have to do our bit."

Alice said that Delia had come to talk about her share of the hall.

"What, is she dumb?" Reggie shrieked. "Why do you have to speak for her? Whose mother are you, mine or Delia's?"

"What is it you wish to discuss, darling?" Gwen said, taking Delia by the arm.

Stephen said that the presence of the three sisters reminded him of a fairy tale, which one he was not sure, but there were several, weren't there, with a youngest of three who turned out to be the most beautiful and good and kind. He drew Reggie to him and then Gwen, who had hold of Delia. There was a brief struggle, and then Delia tore herself away. To her acute embarrassment Stephen shouted with laughter.

"Delia? What are you here for?" Reggie too was struggling to be free. "You and the old man have quarrelled, haven't you?"

"I wouldn't say they've quarrelled," said Alice.

"No?"

"It must seem so," said Delia, "in outward appearance."

"And you're now living where?"

"She's in the Piercy Castle caravan site," said Alice, aware that her daughter already knew the answers to her questions.

"Why on earth did you go there?"

"She was doing what she was told," said Alice.

"Mother, can't she speak?"

"Come, ladies, ladies!" Stephen clapped his hands. "We'll go up to the library and discuss the long-term plans, and Delia can put her case."

Reggie said, "You had no need to go to a caravan site under any circumstances. I mean, did you think you'd get more out of him that way? Is that what you thought? You're so cunning, little Delia. Funny little ways you've got. You were always the favourite, weren't you. Apple of his eye and so forth. It seemed so unfair, but you were here and we weren't. And you were a pretty little thing, I'll say that. And you're very pretty now, though God knows you could do with taking in hand. Where do you find those clothes? Charity shops? But I'll admit my girls are envious. 'Why can't I look like Aunt Delia? Why can't I talk like her? Why can't I walk like her?' 'What,' I say, 'like this?'" Reggie slammed along the servants' hall in grotesque imitation of tall, slim, fast-moving Delia. "Just as well they're at school instead of here or we might have trouble. We've got to get things settled before the Christmas holidays. Meantime, what are we going to do with her?" she called from the end of the room.

"You can leave her alone, for a start," Tom said surprisingly.

"Oh, who's this, then?"

"This is my friend Tom Charlton," Delia said.

"He's working in the library, aren't you, Tom?" said Stephen Wilson.

Gwen said, "He's very very kindly helping to catalogue the library and assess the state of all the books, at my request, and he's going to research material for a brochure, aren't you, Tom. Mother, we haven't introduced Tom Charlton. Tom, I don't think you've met my mother . . ."

"My mother you know already." Delia smiled at him when the introduction was over and he sat down beside her. "Why are you swearing? I saw you together at Akeld." Esmé looked back and murmured, "How very sweet you were," and blew her nose.

"She wanted to see if she and your father could live there."

"Tom, will you really work for these people?"

But the others were already going up to the cabinet room, off the library, where there was a round leather-topped library table and chairs for everybody. They all sat down and prepared to listen. Stephen spread out his blueprints and estate maps and began to expound. The hall needed reroofing; the limestone slates and Westmorland slates of its older and newer parts had to be taken up and the joists treated before they were relaid. The lead on the roof had to be taken up, melted down, and relaid—a task normally performed every seventy years but delayed now for over a hundred. The guttering had to be replaced and new drains put in throughout. The woodwork of the early sash windows was warped throughout and needed treatment. There was extensive dry rot in the rafters over the main gallery. In sum, repairs to the main house and redecoration would cost over a million pounds. The rest of the fabric might cost another half million to restore. When the assets were totted up, rents raised, and surplus property sold, they would still have to find upwards of three quarters of a million pounds before opening the hall to the public at a much increased fee.

Alice nodded at Delia. "There, you see, the Quondams have always been broke."

"Not exactly hungry, though," Tom said very quietly.

So where was the money to come from, Stephen asked, raising his voice to drown the interruptions. He banged his papers on the table in front of him. Present income from the estate was limited. Anthony had not developed the pheasant and partridge shooting to a standard attractive to syndicates. The farming and forestry paid for themselves and that was about all. "But we've just had some pretty brilliant news. We've all heard talk for years of a new road, a new motorway, to be introduced between Tyne and Humber and the south. Motorways need vast quantities of gravel for their foundation . . ."

At the end of his talk he looked around expectantly. Gwen and Reggie looked bright. Alice and Delia and her mother were frowning. Stephen added, "At a time when we're going into Europe, which is also a time of recession locally, we have to think of attracting money to the area. We have to think of attracting *conferences*. We have to think of attracting *businessmen on entertainment allowances.* The Dutch. The Germans. The Italians. Even the French. The Americans and Japanese who want to do business in Europe. And in due time the Russians. All those who love to confer on commercial themes in pastoral surroundings. It's interesting, isn't it, how businessmen like trees and fields with a few cows dotted on them. Now I've no doubt, no doubt, no doubt that the Chief Planning Officer will go along with us. As a matter of fact, greatly daring, I've spoken to him already, just to put him in the picture, and he was most interested. It's the sort of thing the Prime Minister is out to encourage, isn't it? Now let's look at these maps." He opened them out and spread them over the table. Gwen stood up to help him. For a moment their arms touched. Reggie watched them with a half smile. When all was ready, Stephen began to go over his schemes in more detail.

"What's he talking about?" Delia asked Tom in a whisper. He whispered back. When she understood, she demanded in a loud voice, "Do you mean to tell us that you're in favour of launching a huge gravel extraction enterprise between Hartland and Clum?"

Stephen nodded, glad to have made his point so easily. "We're going to revive the quarrying that has always been carried out in this area . . ."

". . . creating lots of new jobs," said Gwen.

"Oh, absolutely."

"In the village?" asked Delia.

"Most of the work will be done by Walkett Brewer's present work force and their affiliates and, of course, their vast machinery, which does not require a big labour force. There may be work for local lorry drivers. We have to work out these details."

"What lorry drivers do you mean?"

"The ones who'll shift the gravel, Tom."

"Shift the gravel where?"

"As I explained to you yesterday, from the pit workings to the motorway site, routing it east through the village."

"So you'll have heavy vehicles rumbling through Hartland all through the day. How many?"

"Yes, how many?" demanded Delia.

"Another detail to be worked out, Delia. They're projecting an extraction figure of around one hundred and twenty thousand tons of gravel per year, with an aim of finding two million tons in the long haul. At the end of the day, that will work out at . . ." Here Stephen fiddled with his pocket calculator. ". . . some fifty to sixty lorries per diem over fifteen to twenty years. Just a rough figure."

The meeting sat in silence, digesting the information.

At last Alice said, "How much profit do Walkett Brewer stand to make?"

"Ninety percent of what we make. That is, we'll charge ten percent commission and anticipate a gain of roughly two million pounds."

"At ten percent?"

"Correct, Alice."

"There's bound to be trouble in the village," Gwen said. "Everyone is extremely conservative. No one here likes change."

"We could cut them in on the profits, make it a cooperative venture, and so forth. They'd like that. It's their village too, after all."

Tom honked briefly in agreement, but Stephen waved him down. "Absolutely not, Alice, too complicated. Besides, it wouldn't bring in the amount of money we need to raise for the hall. No, if we do this, we do it as a trust for the hall. The village will stand to gain indirectly, of course. From a flood of visitors to the hall who would go shopping in the village afterwards and stay at local hostelries, that sort of thing. We might think of launching a summer music festival in due course."

"With fifty lorries a day pounding up and down the village street?"

"Delia, good point, we might consider putting in a by-road. On the other hand, that'll take up every penny of profit to the estate for the first two years."

"And the rest of the countryside? Will there be anything left of it?"

"Now there you have a point, Esmé. There is bound to be a giant mess. So I've drawn up a quick sketch of what we might promise to do as the extraction gets under way—which of course it won't do for at least a couple of years, as we draw up plans and get them through the planning authorities and environmental protection agencies of various sorts." Stephen handed out blueprints, holding his blazer to his stomach to prevent its getting dusty. "Here we have a projection of what the site will look like eventually. Here's Hartland, here is the site, you see, just south of Clum Abbey. Our farm starts here, on the edge."

"Your father's going to be upset by this, Stephen," Alice observed. "Have you told him?"

"Not yet. He'll go along with us. No trouble. So instead of the present rather boring bottomland, where, by the way, the soil is very very poor, we'll have a lake half a mile long edged with hardwood plantations, a golf course curved round the end of the lake, here, and, prettily concealed, some really snappy post-modern buildings for a leisure centre."

"A leisure centre! Are you serious?"

"Of course, Delia." Stephen smiled patiently. "Do you want people to go on sitting in the Golden Fleece playing shuffleboard and backgammon for the rest of their lives? You have to give something to the neighbourhood in exchange for what you are going to take from it. This will have to be a high-price private club with a proper fence, its own guards, a check-point for vehicles, squash courts, a swimming pool, tennis courts, a gym, a bar . . . you name it."

"Can't imagine the village people in that sort of club."

"He's not having 'village people' in there, love," Tom explained.

"You mean that village people will be excluded from this club of yours?"

"It's not my club, Delia," said Stephen, "it's a Quondam enterprise and a Walkett Brewer enterprise. If village people choose to pay the fees, of course they can join. You see, Tom, we cannot have leisure facilities for everybody simply because they live nearby. It would turn into Bridlington or Blackpool."

"What you want is a Disneyland, like the one near Paris." Alice spoke bitterly.

"Hardly." But Stephen did not take offence. "Not a Disneyland, no. You're being naughty." He smiled at Alice as if she had designed French Disneyland herself. "No, we have to control the development. We mustn't let it get away from us. Or we'll have something monstrous on our doorstep."

There was a long and tremulous silence in which everyone fingered the maps and sketches and projections.

Then Esmé said nervously, "In spite of what you say, Stephen, that is good bottomland that you're referring to, and it seems very sad that it should not go back to farmland when the gravel extraction is finished."

"But there will be no topsoil there, Esmé. We will have to remove the topsoil."

This news took its time to sink in.

"No topsoil?" Alice questioned in a bewildered voice.

After a pause, Esmé said, "I was thinking that quite apart from the quarrying it is a fearful thing to reduce good farms to mere golf courses and tennis courts."

But Stephen had an answer to everything—an agreement, a rejoinder, a contradiction, all equally smooth and acceptable. Now he appeared to lament his own necessities. "Yes, that happened in the Lothians, didn't it, Esmé, when cheap overseas wheat arrived here in the eighties of the last century; they converted many a world-famous farm in East Lothian to golf courses. A great shame."

"So must we too . . ."

"Ah, but we're quarrying first, aren't we, Esmé, the golf course will be very much a secondary installation, made to cover up the inevitable eyesore." Stephen looked as if he had made an unanswerable point.

Esmé frowned. "An eyesore, yes, an eyesore." They all looked at her in surprise.

"Do tell me if I'm wrong," said Delia eventually, "but your idea is to destroy the landscape by gouging its surface and digging out layers and layers of underlying material, the gravel, till it all looks raw and muddy, and you'd take out this gravel by the lorryload, creating a flow of lorries that will thunder to and fro through our village day after day, and you will turn the scar afterward into a sort of exclusive country club, so that ordinary people will completely lose out? All for the sake of a quite moderate amount of money."

"Several million pounds!"

"We'll get planning permission for this, of course?" Gwen asked.

"How long will the quarrying go on?" Delia interrupted.

"In the first instance, twenty years."

"And in the second instance?"

"Another twenty years. That's to say, Walkett Brewer will have an option on the second span of time."

"You know that conservation is a luxury?" Reggie asked.

"Then we are luxuries too, Reggie," Delia said. "The hall is a luxury and everyone in it."

"She means that we shouldn't be too commercial," Alice said. "I understand that. We mustn't be greedy, I think that's what Delia is saying."

"Absolutely." Stephen looked around the table expectantly, but no one quite understood if he was agreeing and no one met his eyes.

Esmé put her hand on Delia's.

"I think it's brilliant," said Reggie finally.

"Obscene, you mean, don't you."

"Oh, Delia darling, don't speak like that!" cried Alice. "Nothing's decided yet, is it, Gwennie?"

"Of course it isn't." Gwen smiled. "She does get excited, doesn't she?" She spoke quite fondly, leaning across the table to Esmé and even reaching out a hand, which Esmé ignored.

"You've got to admit it's a simply brilliant idea," Stephen said.

"Everything we do is done at a price," Gwen said unctuously.

"The unfortunate truth is that these problems have to be shared among the community," Stephen continued. "We will each have to accept our share. The development will affect our farm at Clum. Clum will look right down on the operation. Someone noticed that already, I think. Was it you, Tom? But I say this: if an operator comes along with a viable plan of creating wealth on a national scale, at the end of the day some people are bound to be unhappy."

"*Unhappy?*" Delia cried. "You're going to destroy our lives, the lives of everyone in the village and the valley, and our homes, and the countryside, and the environment, and you say some of us are going to be *unhappy?*" She sprang up and ran out of the room. In a moment Alice rose and followed her. The rest sat on in silence, in the certain knowledge that Stephen would soon resume.

"*Jesus.*"

Reggie bristled. She addressed everyone but Tom. "Let me bring this up here and now. I mean, if we're having total strangers sitting in on our meetings, I'd have made sure Jeremy sat in too. He's family. And he has *years* of experience in business matters. And Gwen, you could have asked Billy. I thought Billy was going to do most of the restoration anyway? What's happened to that idea?"

"Billy is terribly keen, of course. He's a craftsman."

"He should be here then. Not strangers."

"Tom is deeply involved. And this is just a beginning," soothed Stephen. "A preliminary. We wanted someone outside the family to raise the questions we might overlook. Delia will come round. I wouldn't worry about her, Esmé. The young are so absolute."

"I'm not worrying. Besides, Alice has taken her on."

Alice caught up with Delia in the entrance hall, where she had paused to see who was hurrying after her. "Delia, I had no idea . . ."

"I'm sure you didn't. But Alice, I have to give this back to you. Believe me, I'm very very grateful." She scrabbled in her pocket and drew out the bank notes and cheque that Alice had given her the previous evening and gave the bunch to Alice.

"But why are you giving it back? You need it. I'm glad to give it to you."

"I don't know. It just seems wrong. I know you're not to blame, but you are their mother. I really can't . . . Look, I wonder where Father is. I must find him. How dark it is."

"Very well." Alice stuffed the money inside her bag. "I'll continue to think of it as your money, and any time you need it, ask for it."

"That's kind, but . . . I have to find Dad."

Alice did her best to be sensible. "He's probably at the Aytons'. You try there, I'll see if Mrs. Thwaite knows. If I find him, I'll tell him where you are and that you're looking for him. He'll be very pleased."

They hurried off in different directions. Alice felt full of gloom. There was no one about in the salon or the gallery or the ballroom, and in the family wing only Mrs. Thwaite, cutting up vegetables at the kitchen table. "You need a better knife than that, Mrs. Thwaite," said Alice professionally. "I must send you one. Oh, have you seen Mr. Quondam?"

She had not.

"Delia is looking for him at the Aytons'. You know he's there with Esmé, don't you? Why, I don't understand. Frankly everything is pretty chaotic at the moment."

Mrs. Thwaite looked distressed. "Mr. Quondam has been acting very strange since she left. He shot his dogs, you know."

"What on earth for? Anthony shot his dogs? My blood runs cold."

"Then there's this quarrying business Gwen told me about. I don't like the sound of that. Mr. Quondam would not agree to it if he was to live here still. I said to Gwen, 'Your father can't approve of that.' She says it's not his to worry about anymore."

"Oh, Mrs. Thwaite! We have to try and work this one out. Forgive me running off, I have to find Anthony."

The barn held more clutter than ever. Delia's things were still neatly bundled in a heap near the door. Most of Anthony's and Esmé's necessities had gone to the Aytons', but in their place were mountains of furniture and trunks that were probably Reggie's, sent on from Harrogate. There was no sign of Delia, so Alice started through the gardens on the way to the Aytons', at the far end of the village. She was careless now of being recognised.

As she approached the flower gardens she saw in the distance the hall gardener, William Sykes, toiling to and fro with the wheelbarrow carting loads from the compost heap to the flower beds. In the famous double border, his assistant, Patsy Muir, forked the compost over the cut-down clumps of asters and delphiniums and lupins and chrysanthemums, and around the rose bushes. When they had emptied the compost heap they would begin distributing the manure that had been dumped near the pavilion. The flowers of Quondam Hall were a model of harmonious forms and colours. Alice, who had found the hall itself intractable, loved the garden from the start and in her day had maintained it pretty much as she inherited it from Lady Stella. When the old gardener died, it was Alice who had found William Sykes, then a passionate youth working unhappily as a cowman, and put him to work among the flowers. So the garden survived Esmé's lack of interest. As Alice approached over the lawn she admired the distant labouring figures. They appeared to be pushing on as hard as they could in order to reap the benefit of the coming rain. Rain would wash the good of the compost and manure into the soil and start the process of enrichment that would result in more and better flowers in the spring.

Dark clouds congregated over the high wood. The green of the parkland was livid. The cattle had been taken into the farmyard that afternoon, so they didn't dot the grassland in the preferred manner. The beck that meandered towards the hall was full and would be fuller, flooding gently from the last ford in the village up to the roadway and easing the violence of motorbikes. And what of Patsy Muir, the young woman desperately forking in the flower beds, what was she to William Sykes the gardener proper? Why did she stay doing labourer's work in a quiet Yorkshire village? Alice had met her only once, a day or two ago. What were young women up to, these days?

The prevalent west wind had been jostling through the woods for some days. Now it drove piles of leaves out of walled corners where they had accumulated and knocked over bicycles propped outside the post office and the grocer's in Hartland and lifted a corrugated iron roof off one of the hall's outlying sheds that should have been roofed with pantiles long ago, and later made a last rafter crack on an old stone hut in the fields so that its roof caved in. Rooks blew about the sky like the black plastic bags left by the rubbish men. The big hollies glittered on the edge of the woods. Men working in the depths of the woods cried off their work for fear of falling timber. Then came rain in gusts, blanking out windows, sheeting over roads, pouring across the tar of thin lanes, glistening in the furrows of winter wheat.

At last, lightning cut off the power supply to Hartland, and Alice, sheltering for a moment in the pavilion to put a scarf over her head, saw some of the hall windows go dark. No doubt the meeting in the cabinet room would break up because no one could see to read. Then she saw that the gardeners were putting their forks in the wheelbarrow. Patsy Muir's hair lay in streaks over her face and head. Anthony and Delia appeared without seeing Alice and walked across the lawn with their streaming faces pointing in the direction of the park. They paused and spoke briefly to the gardeners. Anthony gestured as he talked, the way a man gestured describing something he'd lost. A figure on a horse hurried through the park on the way to the village and shelter. Presently Anthony and Delia passed through the wicket gate into the park, the gardeners gazing after them. Rain continued falling in sheets. It would be torrential, to judge from the clouds. Father and daughter wore waterproof jackets and Wellingtons but no hats. Alice thought that torrential rain demanded hats. She was well accoutered, herself, in her warm raincoat and her boots and scarf. When she neared the outer door in the garden wall, she looked back. Where on earth were Anthony and Delia going? The figures were nearly in the lee of the high woods now. Suddenly the figure of Tom Charlton appeared in the distance, hastening after them along the far side of the stream that picked its way through the park.

There was no need to worry, then. They would sort things out for themselves. Alice found her car in the courtyard and set off for Clum.

Esmé had left Gwen and Reggie with Stephen as soon as the lights failed and made her way through the gathering dark to Delia's old barn, where she half expected to find Anthony. The barn was empty. She hastily sat down on a cot and made some phone calls. In the first, she was incoherent. Lady Piercy entirely understood. "Esmé, calm down. What new behaviour of his has led you to think that he's now off his head when he wasn't before? He's always been mad. He's always had some marvellous reason for doing something lunatic. For example?—giving away everything, like Tolstoy. But he's not even re-ligious, unlike Tolstoy. And you are no Mrs. Tolstoy fighting with him all the time, are you? You are peaceful and calm. I mean it. Oh, marrying you was mad? Rubbish. And what on earth is the point of worrying about that now, I ask? You say he shot his dogs? Well, I happened to hear of young Jack Coulton the other day, threw his pack of beagles out of the bedroom window. People do strange things. I don't know about blame, Esmé. Don't waste your breath. Call up your doctor immediately and tell him. That is what doctors are for. Let him take over. Ring him immediately. William will be over to see you the moment he gets home. About seven or eight tonight, he said. At the Aytons'? Why the Aytons'?"

The second call was more reassuring. Sally Ayton had been ex-tremely kind to Anthony and Esmé—so kind that Esmé suspected some bottling up of her natural exuberance. She was still kind. Yes, Anthony *had* been in her house, but he'd gone out. Delia had come and they'd fallen on each other's necks and they'd gone out. For a walk. Yes, in the pouring rain and without hats. To talk things over, it seemed.

But then came the worry. "Esmé, love, he was on about his dogs. He said Gwen and Reggie should be shot and buried under the stones of the old quarry in place of his dogs. He said they're more vicious than any dog. 'That's no way to speak of anyone, least of all your children,' I said to him. He said, 'I have no children. One I drove out and the other two have disowned me.' 'And who shot the dogs?' I said. 'Was it you? You shot them. You can't blame Gwen and Reggie for that.' He was just asking for sympathy. I'm blowed if I know what's going on. He's not himself. He's a grown man, I can't keep him in if he wants to go out."

The doctor was less satisfactory. He spoke as if Esmé were the patient rather than Anthony. "You feel uneasy about him, is that it? Talking irrationally, is he? Been under stress, that sort of thing? Does he appear disorientated? Know who he's speaking to? Know the date and the day? Well, if he's gone out, there seems no point in my calling round. At the Aytons'? Why the Aytons' and not the hall? If you could get Mrs. Ayton to give me a ring when he comes back, that would be best."

Esmé called Sally Ayton and passed on the message.

How unfair life was! How lucky Anthony was to have Delia with him. It was years since Delia had been for a walk with her mother. Exhausted, sad, Esmé swung her legs up onto the cot and lay down with her head on the pillow and like Goldilocks fell fast asleep.

Once in her cosy bedroom in the Wilsons' farmhouse at Clum, Alice had a hot bath and changed her clothes. Then she sat down and began a letter. *My dear Bob, I am coming home. Will you be there to meet me? Will you forgive my unpardonable behaviour and the silly things I said? I miss you more than I can say.* What indeed could she say? The rest of the letter was too difficult to write. If she felt up to it, she would write another letter tomorrow. Or Bob might call. Luckily the Wilsons' stationery included a telephone number under the address.

The doctor heard nothing from Sally Ayton about Anthony Quondam, for the very good reason that Anthony and Delia had not come back. At eight o'clock, just before his dinner, his conscience roused him and he called Sally himself. Putting the phone down, he wondered whether the agitation in her voice was justified. No doubt the missing pair had taken shelter from the storm now raging, in some farmhouse, or in a church or barn. On the other hand, if Anthony was half as mad as Sally declared, she might be right to worry. "Keep in touch," the doctor said, aware of his wife's annoyance that once again he had thought of something urgent to do between her announcement that dinner was ready and her actual placing it on the table.

Though the thought of Anthony crossed his mind now and then in the course of the evening, he put it out of his head, and was surprised to get a call from William Piercy at one in the morning. It roused him from a deep sleep, and for an hour he lay awake, limp with fatigue and nightmare, before pulling trousers over pyjamas in the time-honoured fashion and putting on thick socks and Wellington boots and heavy rain gear. Into his bag he'd thrown blood plasma and checked to find the usual things—morphine, splints, bandages—in case those lost in the storm had been knocked down by a falling tree and pinned under it, or had slipped over a ledge or something of the sort. There was a big torch, too, and a small flask of brandy for himself if he was kept out for a long time. He wouldn't have gone out normally till they found the missing people, but this time it was the lord of the bloody manor who'd gone missing. Mrs. Quondam, a fairly nice woman forty years younger than the old man and endowed with a brain the size of a jenny wren, had called him only that afternoon to say her husband had been behaving strangely. He'd wondered at the time what in hell that was supposed to mean. Most people behaved strangely. It was one of life's little secrets. In this case he'd heard something of the old man's troubles and guessed they were accompanied by the common ones of old age—humiliation of body, insult to the brain, loss of memory, disorientation, weakness of muscle. How God-awful old age was, and how little he could do for the old except listen and nod and do that once a week to show them he thought about them. He hoped for Anthony Quondam's sake that he'd die on his wandering in the storm. Not a bad way to go at all. A reasonable way for a countryman. A respectable way for a dear old man, a fine old man. The girl he barely knew, and never as a patient since she was never ill. What on earth was she thinking about, letting him wander off into the woods at his age? But he was a pretty strong old man and probably as stubborn as a mule.

The doctor anticipated spending hours waiting for the search parties to find them. Well, he hadn't exactly hurried, either. As he drove out of his drive he felt the presence of his wife and children. When he returned, his axe-faced wife would be waiting with warm milk and blessed silence and once they'd got into bed again, the warmth of her body. What a stupid thing it was to be a doctor, unable to help people who really needed help, listening to them, observing them, diagnosing, dispensing antibiotics, but really only trying to understand and very seldom succeeding even in that small task; letting them down gently, making them settle for the fifth-rate, failing them.

Once as a novice locum—before the National Health Service had more or less ordained that women should have their babies in hospital—he'd been called out to a breech birth in a home delivery and he'd stalled for four hours, having no idea how to open forceps, let alone use them, and presuming in his ignorance that forceps would be called for. There was no way out. He had to go in the end. The midwife called him four times. The last time he let the phone ring, pretending he was on his way. When he got to the house the child had been born, the mother was in a bad way, and the midwife was ready to report him but she didn't. Somehow they all survived, that was the point. He might as well have gone in the first instance and saved a lot of hysteria. His presence was all that was needed. He used to suffer with that early memory of his cowardice, but he didn't any more. There had been a million failures since then. Every day was a failure. He didn't like this part of England with its sharp class divisions and lack of anyone interested in discussing matters in an educated and disinterested manner. His chief pleasure was playing the cello with three other amateur musicians once a week.

One of the ancient lindens had fallen across the road on one side of the green and blocked it, so he backed up and went round the other way, over lanes littered with branches, up the hill to Howden, the windshield wipers going recklessly, the headlights on tossing branches, the car shoved by the wind and then let go. A couple of trees, oaks by the look of them, had fallen and now partly blocked the road; they had been dragged aside or sawn up to let traffic through. On the side of the lane past Howden Church he came upon cars drawn up on both grass verges, with men under umbrellas and wearing rain gear standing in the road, and when he was a dozen yards off he saw that there was a car upside down below a muddy scar on the embankment. The policeman from Soulby, the next village, came up to his window. The ambulance had apparently come and gone. One of the ladies from the hall was involved, with a man, a friend of hers, no, not a husband. They'd gone after a number of others looking for the lady's father. The shoulder had washed out and they'd been coming along urgently and met another car and had to swerve on to the shoulder. Both left wheels sank with it as it collapsed and they went with it and flipped over.

The doctor wondered if it was Mrs. Smith or Mrs. Bowers, both awesome, bossy creatures, and who the man was. He felt the lick of sexual curiosity. "Conscious, were they? Badly hurt? Hard to tell? Is the lady's husband here? I'll have a word with him. And old Mr. Quondam, have they found him, Charlie?"

"They've found the young lady, sir. At least, William Piercy found her. They were engaged to be married, my wife tells me."

Another car had drawn up behind the doctor. Looking through his rear mirror the doctor recognised the mother in the passenger seat, the doomed Esmé, about to be reduced to yells and screams and sobs and torn hair, but now staring, masked by the glare of headlights—the pop eyes, the pouty mouth, the air of a small valiant lap-dog. Peter Wilson from Clum was driving her. "Look," the doctor said to the policeman, "get that woman out of here while we sort things out."

8

At some point in that dreadful night Tom Charlton told himself that
if he survived he would sell everything he owned and buy an acre or
two in Armadale, on Skye, and grow strawberries and other berries,
and asparagus and fine peas and perhaps artichokes. Armadale faced the
mainland and was sheltered from the prevalent winds from the Atlan-
tic, so the climate was soft and wet and warm enough for palm trees,
and in the twenty-hour days of summer, grass took on a bluish tinge
and became thick and lush as nowhere else. Anything that didn't grow
well out of doors he would grow in plastic tunnels, suitably sheltered
by cliffs and woods. He would sell the produce to big hotels and famous restaurants within a fifty-mile radius, which at the present had
to have stuff freighted from the south. He would make enough to live
on, he was sure. And if anybody asked him why no one had already
done what he thought of doing, he would say that everyone thought
of doing it, but didn't. The Celts were poor husbandmen, he would
say, as well as poor fishermen; they had lost their spirit with the advent
of the potato, or the Union with England, or the failure of the Fifteen
and the Forty-five, or the Clearances, or the Famine, or the decline
of Gaelic. In other words, history was responsible, not lack of talent.
Tom was something of a missionary.

As soon as the funerals were over he drove to Skye in Delia's old car, which Esmé had given him, and stayed with an old woman in Torrin on a croft, where he would hear all the gossip that was so large an entertainment in the long nights of winter. Meanwhile he carried peat turves for the old woman and mended her roof and did her shopping for her in the indispensable car and worked at odd jobs on the island and, most important, made it known why he was there so people could get over their laughter and think seriously of what he was up to. By February he had his eye on a couple of acres in Armadale that a man was thinking of selling, and the long, slow maturation of sale began.

William Piercy came to visit him at Easter and they climbed Ben-na-Cailleach together and built a cairn in memory of Delia and took a photograph of it for Esmé.

Moved by the report of this deed and by tales of Tom's rudeness to the laird when he arrived from London with advice on pest control, the owner of the desirable acres made up his mind about them in May, and soon after offered them to Tom. Tom worked hard on the digging and manuring and planting all through the summer, and the next year had a small successful crop. The year after that, his fruit and vegetable business did well and he rented more land with a view to buying it later. His mother died, leaving him some money, and he bought a bothy near his land as well as a vacant croft-house on the shore, and worked on them during the winter. The croft-house he rented to summer visitors and he left Torrin for the bothy the moment it was habitable. He remembered Delia every day. Sometimes he thought of finding her dead in William's arms. The two of them huddled under a bank, soaked, in the howling drenching dark. Sometimes he thought of her ideal house in the berm and of her grave, the two together. Sometimes he saw her at the tiny window he had installed looking over the narrow sea to the hills on the mainland.

Esmé put the photograph of the cairn in a little frame by her bed at Akeld. Immediately after Anthony and Delia died, she had nowhere to live. She couldn't stay at the Aytons' for more than a day or two. Akeld wasn't finished, and was it hers? She wouldn't live in the hall, and she refused to go away until the legal entanglements were sorted out. So she moved into the best of Hartland's three pubs, where she was a profound embarrassment to Gwen and Reggie. They promptly sent the estate workmen back to Akeld. Esmé busied herself with getting it in order, not caring in her grief what order in particular, but then trying to recall the way she had once conceived of it, out of loyalty to Anthony as much as anything. And then she moved in with all her belongings, including those that Gwen and Reggie had formerly refused to let her have. She let it be known that she intended to stay there always. The story did no harm, though untrue. She lived with dignity and far more comfortably than ever before, and there was plenty of time to announce that Akeld was too isolated for her now that she was alone.

Legally she was in a strong position. Anthony had split the hall and estate among his three daughters, but did not sign the deed of transfer. Then he disinherited Delia so the deed had to be redrawn. This second deed was not signed either. Then he announced that he intended to reinstate Delia and give her a third of the estate, but again he did not sign any document. When he died, the question was whether the estate was regarded as his in its entirety, in which case everything would go to Esmé, or whether the unsigned deed of transfer would be binding. If Esmé owned everything, the question was whether she would boot the stepdaughters out of the hall and take possession of it herself. It was soon decided: in view of the fact that there was a valid will leaving everything to her, Esmé was the sole legatee.

But Esmé was still in a fix. She disliked the hall and she did not wish to punish Gwen and Reggie. She had always felt uncomfortable at the thought of coming between them and their natural inheritance. She therefore arranged for them to keep two thirds of the property, while she kept Delia's share and the controlling interest. Like most new widows, she thought she was destitute, so she felt proud of her generosity. Gwen and Reggie, on the other hand, had worked out that she was still a wealthy woman in her own right, while they had only their shares of the income from the estate to support them. They were therefore less than grateful, and they were irked that they could do nothing with the estate without her approval. Strangely enough, they also found that she had an ally in Billy Bowers. He was as gentle as she was, but turned into a tiger by jealousy of Stephen Wilson. And he'd been made tigerish also by the death of Jeremy in the car crash on the night of the storm. Chaos loomed: as the sole adult male in the family, he believed he *had* to step forward.

So the restoration of the hall with a view to its public opening went ahead. The lawyers set up a trust: the three women were in control; Billy Bowers and Stephen Wilson were advisers. But where was the money to come from to restore the place satisfactorily and to instal the cafeteria, the restaurant, and the shop? "I think we should shelve the gravel extraction project for the time being," Esmé declared in the first meeting of the trust after the catastrophe.

"But where is the money coming from if not from there?" Reggie asked.

"The money for the hall? Oh, there's the income from the estate, and our investments, and grants. Perhaps Stephen could look into the possibility of grants?"

Stephen appeared gratified. "What a businesswoman you are, Esmé!"

The sisters glanced at each other. Was he ironic? Ironic as well as toothsome? "Meanwhile we're going ahead with our development of Hartland, agreed? We must insist on matching shop fronts, and that covenant shopkeepers and tenants maintain the same colour of flowers in window-boxes and limit the range of colour for doors and windows. Then there's provision for cars. I'm seeing the council on Monday about a three-hundred-car park beyond the graveyard. We've had applications from Laura Ashley, Thornleys Country Clothing, a video shop, another gift shop, and three mill outlets, together with one from a boutique in Leeds."

"You're so good at this."

"Esmé! Flattery will get you nowhere!"

Gwen cut through the flirtation. She said she wished the gravel extraction project hadn't been pushed aside so summarily. She saw it as the salvation of Hartland. But she spoke in an unusually subdued manner.

"Delia didn't think so," said Esmé. "So that's that."

"Such decisiveness, Esmé!"

"Yes. Weird, isn't it." Esmé smiled sheepishly.

Stephen went on: "And then there's the question of the rents, the commercial and private rents in the village. Very low for years, now bringing in much more realistic income."

"Isn't there a question here of noblesse oblige?" Billy Bowers suggested. "For some of the older concerns like the bakery and the haberdashery? And for the older tenants whom the family has known for years? People on very low fixed incomes?"

"More noblesse if you want, but less oblige if you don't mind," Reggie said. "Dad overdid the oblige and just about ruined us. Remember, I've got four girls to educate all by myself and it's not going to be easy, even with Jeremy's life insurance. By the time they're launched, it won't be worth a sixpence. And I'm not like Gwen, with a profession to turn to, and a husband to keep the wolf from the door." She gave poor Billy a bleak smile. "So if the shopkeepers find our rents high, let them charge more for their goods. And as for the tenants who can't afford the rent—well, I don't see why we've got to keep them. I mean, this is not the welfare state we're talking about here." Widowhood had lent her some refinement, pared her down, cut the gaudiness of her clothes, and it took some time for the incongruity of her remarks to sink in.

"Tell me about Jeremy's estate. Did he leave you . . . well, decently off? Forgive me, you are my sister, I do worry . . . We're family here, aren't we." Gwen's solicitude took them aback. Reggie stared. "So tragic, the way the shoulder of the lane collapsed just when we . . . And why was he taken, and not me? I feel guilty, or ashamed, or somehow responsible." Gwen's eyes were full of tears.

"Such rubbish!" Stephen took her hand and pressed it to his cheek.

"Stop it," Reggie said. "For God's sake, just stop it!" She left the room and slammed the door behind her.

"I don't know what that was about," said Esmé. "But I don't think it was very pleasant."

"We are all still grief stricken," Stephen said, and pursed his lips.

They lost no time in reducing Delia to size. "I had a look at her stuff in the barn," Reggie said, "and quite honestly I don't think she had anything going for her. She did quite well with that last competition, but that was strictly beginner's work."

"She was a baby. She needed to grow up. She needed to get away from here. She needed the wide world. She needed to get away from people like us," Gwen said.

"What's wrong with people like us?"

"Do you want to know only people like yourself?"

"Yes."

Stephen's family were equally worried about him. His brother, Calvert, said, "I put nothing past Stephen," and when his father demurred, said that Stephen had always been dead jealous. "You'd be blind not to realise what Stephen's up to."

"You mean, Stephen would ruin the valley out of personal pique?"

"He'd never admit to that, would he, even to himself."

"I should hope not."

"Stephen knows he's your son. You know that, don't you? He never made much of it. He was pretty fond of Mother, that's why. But as for the gravel pit, he knows that people round here want to be as progressive as anyone else. We all get tired of living in a beauty spot. We want to be like other people and make lots of money. So I'm sure there'll be very little objection to the gravel pit. Oh, there'll be a village Hampden or two to speak against it, and someone will start a petition. But Stephen knows the Chief Planning Officer, and now that Anthony's gone and just Esmé and the two sisters are in charge, I see nothing to hold him up."

"And you'll put up with that?" Peter was amazed at his son's intransigence.

"Oh, I'll protest, but there's something about radical change that appeals to people. And Stephen is a plausible man. People trust him. He's out to make you pay, Father, do understand that. As Gwen was out to make her father pay."

"I'm not sure I understand."

"She was always ringing up here after Stephen, that's what I'm saying. She wanted Stephen all to her very own. It's obvious. She's stopped ringing up for the moment, but she may start again at any time."

"I missed that," said Peter Wilson humbly. "And what about poor Billy?"

"Billy can look after himself," Calvert said to his father's surprise.

The view at dusk from Alice's window was all she'd said it was: the looming dark mass of the treetops, only just now coming into leaf, some of them netted with points of light, all threaded beneath with car lights winking red and streaming white; the great tall buildings on the skyline with their decks of illuminated windows. Esmé stood exhilarated on Alice's balcony. With her were Alice's three cats, all intent on hurling themselves to the street eight storeys below. What with keeping them off the balustrade and resisting the keen March wind, Esmé felt at the mercy of the elements.

"Come in, for God's sake," Alice said, opening the French windows.

The cats rushed in with Esmé. They had taken a fancy to her. Her black dress showed every hair. A thick black cat with lop ears sat happily on her knee. Two like small snow tigers rushed round and round her chair crying in strange raucous cat voices. All three were evidently of rare and costly species.

"You have the right touch," shrieked Alice over the racket. She shut the cats in the kitchen and said in a normal tone of voice, "I can't tell you how much it means to me to see you here. It's been awful, even for me, though Bob has been wonderful. I don't know what I'd have done without him. What it's been like for you I can't imagine. Tell me, frankly, do you *get on* with my daughters? Are they *kind* to you? Do they *look after* you?"

Esmé thought of her triumphs. "Sufficiently well."

"You have been very generous, Esmé."

"I don't know about getting on with them. They'd like me out of the way. They're *determined* to push through the gravel extraction scheme and ruin our lives. They will probably win, too. I very much hope Robert has some good advice for me; I'm so much looking forward to meeting him, Alice. So very kind of him to offer his expertise."

"He's coming prepared. He says you must protect yourself. And the village, of course. And the hall."

"I will lose in the end."

"Surely everyone is on your side. They'll rally round you. After all that has happened, they're bound to. What does Peter Wilson say?"

"Peter has cancer. He's not really available."

"I can't bear it, Esmé."

"You see, I think we are doomed. Do you know, even if Anthony had not died that night, the night of the storm, they were planning to have him declared incompetent?—shortly after he'd signed the transfer deed, of course."

"They couldn't do that."

"Oh yes. I'd put nothing past them. But he was not mad, Alice. He was only suffering from indignation. If only Delia . . ."

"If only she'd not got involved?"

"Yes."

"I've always thought that you must allow people to fulfil their natures. You couldn't stop her. I couldn't stop Gwen and Reggie. I certainly couldn't stop Anthony."

"But what about fulfilling *my* nature?" asked Esmé. "I'm sick of other people's fulfilment."

"My dear, I do see. Do you know what Anthony said to me when we finally broke up? 'You never were any good for me,' he said, in the bitterest voice. 'So what,' I thought, though wounded to the quick; he wasn't exactly good for me, either. I did my best."

"That's never enough," said Esmé. "As we know." She smiled radiantly, and Alice, after a moment's reflection, smiled radiantly back.

"We've planted new oaks at Akeld," Esmé said, and the buzzer sounded. It was the doorman announcing a visitor.

"That can't be Bob yet—and of course he has his own key. Who is it?" Alice called down the intercom. "I can't make out a word. Someone for Mrs. Quondam, well, naturally. I can't get the name. Oh, someone for you, Esmé? Sorry. Send him up. Esmé, I didn't realise . . ."

"I'm here for three days, then I'm off to see my brother Roderick in Barbados for a week," said Esmé while they awaited the visitor.

But who is this gentleman she has in tow, Alice wondered. Of course, she is still young and good-looking. Why shouldn't she have an admirer? But when the doorbell sounded and she went to answer it, she was astonished to find Stephen Wilson, with his familiar smile.